Four Ghost Stories by Mary Louisa Molesworth

Mary Louisa Molesworth, née Stewart was born in Rotterdam, Holland on May 29th, 1839.

She was educated in Great Britain and Switzerland with much of her early life spent in Manchester, where her Father had gained wealth as a merchant.

In 1861 she married Major R. Molesworth but the marriage was to end in a legal separation in 1879.

Mary wrote for adults with such works as Lover and Husband (1869) and Cicely (1874), appearing under her pseudonym of Ennis Graham.

She is best known as the writer of books for older children such as Tell Me a Story (1875), Carrots (1876), The Cuckoo Clock (1877), The Tapestry Room (1879), and A Christmas Child (1880). She has been called "the Jane Austen of the nursery," and The Carved Lions (1895) is hailed as her masterpiece.

Typical of the time, her young child characters often use a lisping style, and words may be misspelt to better represent a child—"jography" for geography.

One of many authors at the time to experiment with supernatural fiction she published collections in 1888 and 1896.

Mary Louisa Molesworth died on January 20th, 1921 and is buried at Brompton Cemetery in London.

Index of Contents

I

LADY FARQUHAR'S OLD LADY

A TRUE GHOST STORY

"One that was a woman, sir; but, rest her soul, she's dead."

I myself have never seen a ghost (I am by no means sure that I wish ever to do so), but I have a friend whose experience in this respect has been less limited than mine. Till lately, however, I had never heard the details of Lady Farquhar's adventure, though the fact of there being a ghost story which she could, if she chose, relate with the authority of an eye-witness, had been more than once alluded to before me.

Living at extreme ends of the country, it is but seldom my friend and I are able to meet; but a few months ago I had the good fortune to spend some days in her house, and one evening our conversation happening to fall on the subject of the possibility of so-called "supernatural" visitations or communications, suddenly what I had heard returned to my memory.

"By the bye," I exclaimed, "we need not go far for an authority on the question. You have seen a ghost yourself, Margaret. I remember once hearing it alluded to before you, and you did not contradict it. I have so often meant to ask you for the whole story. Do tell it to us now."

Lady Farquhar hesitated for a moment, and her usually bright expression grew somewhat graver. When she spoke, it seemed to be with a slight effort.

"You mean what they all call the story of 'my old lady,' I suppose," she said at last. "Oh yes, if you care to hear it, I will tell it you. But there is not much to tell, remember."

"There seldom is in true stories of the kind," I replied. "Genuine ghost stories are generally abrupt and inconsequent in the extreme, but on this very account all the more impressive. Don't you think so?"

"I don't know that I am a fair judge," she answered. "Indeed," she went on rather gravely, "my own opinion is that what you call true ghost stories are very seldom told at all."

"How do you mean? I don't quite understand you," I said, a little perplexed by her words and tone.

"I mean," she replied, "that people who really believe they have come in contact with—with anything of that kind, seldom care to speak about it."

"Do you really think so? do you mean that you feel so yourself?" I exclaimed with considerable surprise. "I had no idea you did, or I would not have mentioned the subject. Of course you know I would not ask you to tell it if it is the least painful or disagreeable to you to talk about it."

"But it isn't. Oh no, it is not nearly so bad as that," she replied, with a smile. "I cannot really say that it is either painful or disagreeable to me to recall it, for I cannot exactly apply either of those words to the thing itself. All that I feel is a sort of shrinking from the subject, strong enough to prevent my ever alluding to it lightly or carelessly. Of all things, I should dislike to have a joke made of it. But with you I have no fear of that. And you trust me, don't you? I don't mean as to truthfulness only; but you don't think me deficient in common sense and self-control—not morbid, or very apt to be run away with by my imagination?"

"Not the sort of person one would pick out as likely to see ghosts?" I replied. "Certainly not. You are far too sensible and healthy and vigorous. I can't, very readily, fancy you the victim of delusion of any kind. But as to ghosts—are they or are they not delusions? There lies the question! Tell us your experience of them, any way."

So she told the story I had asked for—told it in the simplest language, and with no exaggeration of tone or manner, as we sat there in her pretty drawing-room, our chairs drawn close to the fire, for it was Christmas time, and the weather was "seasonable." Two or three of Margaret's children were in the room, though not within hearing of us; all looked bright and cheerful, nothing mysterious. Yet notwithstanding the total deficiency of ghostly accessories, the story impressed me vividly.

"It was early in the spring of '55 that it happened," began Lady Farquhar; "I never forget the year, for a reason I will tell you afterwards. It is fully fifteen years ago now—a long time—but I am still quite able to recall the feeling this strange adventure of mine left on me, though a few details and particulars have grown confused and misty. I think it often happens so when one tries, as it were too hard, to be accurate and unexaggerated in telling over anything. One's very honesty is against one. I have not told it over many times, but each time it seems more difficult to tell it quite exactly; the impression left at the time was so powerful that I have always dreaded incorrectness or exaggeration creeping in. It reminds me, too, of the curious way in which a familiar word or name grows distorted, and then cloudy and strange, if one looks at it too long or thinks about it too much. But I must get on with my story. Well, to begin again. In the winter of '54-'55 we were living—my mother, my sisters, and I, that is, and from time to time my brother—in, or rather near, a quiet little village on the south coast of Ireland. We had gone there, before the worst of the winter began at home, for the sake of my health. I had not been as well as usual for some time (this was greatly owing, I believe, to my having lately endured unusual anxiety of mind), and my dear mother dreaded the cold weather for me, and determined to avoid it. I say that I had had unusual anxiety to bear, still it was not of a kind to render me morbid or fanciful. And what is even more to the point, my mind was perfectly free from prepossession or association in connection with the place we were living in, or the people who had lived there before us. I simply knew nothing whatever of these people, and I had no sort of fancy about the house—that it was haunted, or anything of that kind; and indeed I never heard that it was thought to be haunted. It did not look like it; it was just a moderate-sized, somewhat old-fashioned country, or rather sea-side, house, furnished, with the exception of one room, in an ordinary enough modern style. The exception was a small room on the bedroom floor, which, though not locked off (that is to say, the key was left in the lock outside), was not given up for our use, as it was crowded with musty old furniture, packed closely together, and all of a fashion many, many years older than that of the contents of the rest of the house. I remember some of the pieces of furniture still, though I think I was only once or twice in the room all the time we were there. There were two or three old-fashioned cabinets or bureaux; there was a regular four-post bedstead, with the gloomy curtains still hanging round it; and ever so many spider-legged chairs and rickety tables; and I rather think in one corner there was a spinet. But there was nothing particularly curious or attractive, and we never thought of meddling with the things or 'poking about,' as girls sometimes do; for we always thought it was by mistake that this room had not been locked off altogether, so that no one should meddle with anything in it.

"We had rented the house for six months from a Captain Marchmont, a half-pay officer, naval or military, I don't know which, for we never saw him, and all the negotiations were managed by an agent. Captain Marchmont and his family, as a rule, lived at Ballyreina all the year round—they found it cheap and healthy, I suppose—but this year they had preferred to pass the winter in some livelier neighbourhood, and they were very glad to let the house. It never occurred to us to doubt our landlord's being the owner of it: it was not till some time after we left that we learned that he himself was only a tenant, though a tenant of long standing. There were no people about to make friends with, or to hear local gossip from. There were no gentry within visiting distance, and if there had been, we should hardly have cared to make friends for so short a time as we were to be there. The people of the village were mostly fishermen and their families; there were so many of them, we never got to know any specially. The doctor and the priest and the Protestant clergyman were all newcomers, and all three very uninteresting. The clergyman used to dine with us sometimes, as my brother had had some sort of introduction to him when we came to Ballyreina; but we never heard anything about the place from him. He was a great talker, too; I am sure he would have told us anything he knew. In short, there was nothing romantic or suggestive either about our house or the village. But we didn't care. You see we had gone there simply for rest and quiet and pure air, and we got what we wanted.

"Well, one evening about the middle of March I was up in my room dressing for dinner, and just as I had about finished dressing, my sister Helen came in. I remember her saying as she came in, 'Aren't you ready yet, Maggie? Are you making yourself extra smart for Mr. Conroy?' Mr. Conroy was the clergyman; he was dining with us that night. And then Helen looked at me and found fault with me, half in fun of course, for not having put on a prettier dress. I remember I said it was good enough for Mr. Conroy, who was no favourite of mine; but Helen wasn't satisfied till I agreed to wear a bright scarlet neck-ribbon of hers, and she ran off to her room to fetch it. I followed her almost immediately. Her room and mine, I must, by the bye, explain, were at extreme ends of a passage several yards in length. There was a wall on one side of this passage, and a balustrade overlooking the staircase on the other. My room was at the end nearest the top of the staircase. There were no doors along the passage leading to Helen's room, but just beside her door, at the end, was that of the unused room I told you of, filled with the old furniture. The passage was lighted from above by a skylight—I mean, it was by no means dark or shadowy—and on the evening I am speaking of, it was still clear daylight. We dined early at Ballyreina; I don't think it could have been more than a quarter to five when Helen came into my room. Well, as I was saying, I followed her almost immediately, so quickly that as I came out of my room I was in time to catch sight of her as she ran along the passage, and to see her go into her own room. Just as I lost sight of her—I was coming along more deliberately, you understand—suddenly, how or when exactly I cannot tell, I perceived another figure walking along the passage in front of me. It was a woman, a little thin woman, but though she had her back to me, something in her gait told me she was not young. She seemed a little bent, and walked feebly. I can remember her dress even now with the most perfect distinctness. She had a gown of gray clinging stuff, rather scanty in the skirt, and one of those funny little old-fashioned black shawls with a sewed-on border, that you seldom see nowadays. Do you know the kind I mean? It was a narrow, shawl-pattern border, and there was a short tufty black fringe below the border. And she had a gray poke bonnet, a bonnet made of silk 'gathered' on to a large stiff frame; 'drawn' bonnets they used to be called. I took in all these details of her dress in a moment, and even in that moment I noticed too that the materials of her clothes looked good, though so plain and old-fashioned. But somehow my first impulse when I saw her was to call out, 'Fraser, is that you?' Fraser was my mother's maid: she was a young woman, and not the least like the person in front of me, but I think a vague idea rushed across my mind that it might be Fraser dressed up to trick the other servants. But the figure took no notice of my exclamation; it, or she, walked on quietly, not even turning her head round in the least; she walked slowly down the passage, seemingly quite unconscious of my presence, and, to my extreme amazement, disappeared into the unused room. The key, as I think I told you, was always turned in the lock—that is to say, the door was locked, but the key was left in it; but the old woman did not seem to me to unlock the door, or even to turn the handle. There seemed no obstacle in her way: she just quietly, as it were, walked through the door. Even by this time I hardly think I felt frightened. What I had seen had passed too quickly for me as yet to realise its strangeness. Still I felt perplexed and vaguely uneasy, and I hurried on to my sister's room. She was standing by the toilet-table, searching for the ribbon. I think I must have looked startled, for before I could speak she called out, 'Maggie, whatever is the matter with you? You look as if you were going to faint.' I asked her if she had heard anything, though it was an inconsistent question, for to my ears there had been no sound at all. Helen answered, 'Yes:' a moment before I came into the room she had heard the lock of the lumber-room (so we called it) door click, and had wondered what I could be going in there for. Then I told her what I had seen. She looked a little startled, but declared it must have been one of the servants.

"'If it is a trick of the servants,' I answered, 'it should be exposed;' and when Helen offered to search through the lumber-room with me at once, I was very ready to agree to it. I was so satisfied of the reality of what I had seen, that I declared to Helen that the old woman, whoever she was, must be in the room; it stood to reason that, having gone in, she must still be there, as she could not possibly have come out again without our knowledge.

"So, plucking up our courage, we went to the lumber-room door. I felt so certain that but a moment before, some one had opened it, that I took hold of the knob quite confidently and turned it, just as one always does to open a door. The handle turned, but the door did not yield. I stooped down to see why; the reason was plain enough: the door was still locked, locked as usual, and the key in the lock! Then Helen and I stared at each other: her mind was evidently recurring to the sound she had heard; what I began to think I can hardly put in words.

"But when we got over this new start a little, we set to work to search the room as we had intended. And we searched it thoroughly, I assure you. We dragged the old tables and chairs out of their corners, and peeped behind the cabinets and chests of drawers where no one could have been hidden. Then we climbed upon the old bedstead, and shook the curtains till we were covered with dust; and then we crawled under the valances, and came out looking like sweeps; but there was nothing to be found. There was certainly no one in the room, and by all appearances no one could have been there for weeks. We had hardly time to make ourselves fit to be seen when the dinner-bell rang, and we had to hurry downstairs. As we ran down we agreed to say nothing of what had happened before the servants, but after dinner in the drawing-room we told our story. My mother and brother listened to it attentively, said it was very strange, and owned themselves as puzzled as we. Mr. Conroy of course laughed uproariously, and made us dislike him more than ever. After he had gone we talked it over again among ourselves, and my mother, who hated mysteries, did her utmost to explain what I had seen in a matter-of-fact, natural way. Was I sure it was not only Helen herself I had seen, after fancying she had reached her own room? Was I quite certain it was not Fraser after all, carrying a shawl perhaps, which made her look different? Might it not have been this, that, or the other? It was no use. Nothing could convince me that I had not seen what I had seen; and though, to satisfy my mother, we cross-questioned Fraser, it was with no result in the way of explanation. Fraser evidently knew nothing that could throw light on it, and she was quite certain that at the time I had seen the figure, both the other servants were downstairs in the kitchen. Fraser was perfectly trustworthy; we warned her not to frighten the others by speaking about the affair at all, but we could not leave off speaking about it among ourselves. We spoke about it so much for the next few days, that at last my mother lost patience, and forbade us to mention it again. At least she pretended to lose patience; in reality I believe she put a stop to the discussion because she thought it might have a bad effect on our nerves, on mine especially; for I found out afterwards that in her anxiety she even went the length of writing about it to our old doctor at home, and that it was by his advice she acted in forbidding us to talk about it any more. Poor dear mother! I don't know that it was very sound advice. One's mind often runs all the more on things one is forbidden to mention. It certainly was so with me, for I thought over my strange adventure almost incessantly for some days after we left off talking about it."

Here Margaret paused.

"And is that all?" I asked, feeling a little disappointed, I think, at the unsatisfactory ending to the "true ghost story."

"All!" repeated Lady Farquhar, rousing herself as if from a reverie, "all! oh, dear no. I have sometimes wished it had been, for I don't think what I have told you would have left any long-lasting impression on me. All! oh, dear no. I am only at the beginning of my story."

So we resettled ourselves again to listen, and Lady Farquhar continued:—

"For some days, as I said, I could not help thinking a good deal of the mysterious old woman I had seen. Still, I assure you, I was not exactly frightened. I was more puzzled—puzzled and annoyed at not being able in any way to explain the mystery. But by ten days or so from the time of my first adventure the impression was beginning to fade. Indeed, the day before the evening I am now going to tell you of, I don't think my old lady had been in my head at all. It was filled with other things. So, don't you see, the explaining away what I saw as entirely a delusion, a fancy of my own brain, has a weak point here; for had it been all my fancy, it would surely have happened sooner—at the time my mind really was full of the subject. Though even if it had been so, it would not have explained the curious coincidence of my 'fancy' with facts, actual facts of which at the time I was in complete ignorance. It must have been just about ten days after my first adventure that I happened one evening, between eight and nine o'clock, to be alone upstairs in my own room. We had dined at half-past five as usual, and had been sitting together in the drawing-room since dinner, but I had made some little excuse for coming upstairs; the truth being that I wanted to be alone to read over a letter which the evening post (there actually was an evening post at Ballyreina) had brought me, and which I had only had time to glance at. It was a very welcome and dearly-prized letter, and the reading of it made me very happy. I don't think I had felt so happy all the months we had been in Ireland as I was feeling that evening. Do you remember my saying I never forget the year all this happened? It was the year '55 and the month of March, the spring following that first dreadful 'Crimean winter,' and news had just come to England of the Czar's death, and every one was wondering and hoping and fearing what would be the results of it. I had no very near friends in the Crimea, but of course, like every one else, I was intensely interested in all that was going on, and in this letter of mine there was told the news of the Czar's death, and there was a good deal of comment upon it. I had read my letter—more than once, I daresay—and was beginning to think I must go down to the others in the drawing-room. But the fire in my bedroom was very tempting; it was burning so brightly, that though I had got up from my chair by the fireside to leave the room, and had blown out the candle I had read my letter by, I yielded to the inclination to sit down again for a minute or two to dream pleasant dreams and think pleasant thoughts. At last I rose and turned towards the door—it was standing wide open, by the bye. But I had hardly made a step from the fireplace when I was stopped short by what I saw. Again the same strange indefinable feeling of not knowing how or when it had come there, again the same painful sensation of perplexity (not yet amounting to fear) as to whom or what it was I saw before me. The room, you must understand, was perfectly flooded with the firelight; except in the corners, perhaps, every object was as distinct as possible. And the object I was staring at was not in a corner, but standing there right before me—between me and the open door, alas!—in the middle of the room. It was the old woman again, but this time with her face towards me, with a look upon it, it seemed to me, as if she were conscious of my presence. It is very difficult to tell over thoughts and feelings that can hardly have taken any time to pass, or that passed almost simultaneously. My very first impulse this time was, as it had been the first time I saw her, to explain in some natural way the presence before me. I think this says something for my common sense, does it not? My mind did not readily desert matters of fact, you see. I did not think of Fraser this time, but the thought went through my mind, 'She must be some friend of the servants who comes in to see them of an evening. Perhaps they have sent her up to look at my fire.' So at first I looked up at her with simple inquiry. But as I looked my feelings changed. I realised that this was the same being who had appeared so mysteriously once before; I recognised every detail of her dress; I even noticed it more acutely than the first time—for instance, I recollect observing that here and there the short tufty fringe of her shawl was stuck together, instead of hanging smoothly and evenly all round. I looked up at her face. I cannot now describe the features beyond saying that the whole face was refined and pleasing, and that in the expression there was certainly nothing to alarm or repel. It was rather wistful and beseeching, the look in the eyes anxious, the lips slightly parted, as if she were on the point of speaking. I have since thought that if I had spoken, if I could have spoken—for I did make one effort to do so, but no audible words would come at my bidding—the spell that bound the poor soul, this mysterious wanderer from some shadowy borderland between life and death, might have been broken, and the message that I now believe burdened her delivered. Sometimes I wish I could have done it; but then, again—oh no! a voice from those unreal lips would have been too awful—flesh and blood could not have stood it. For another instant I kept my eyes fixed upon her without moving; then there came over me at last with an awful thrill, a sort of suffocating gasp of horror, the consciousness, the actual realisation of the fact that this before me, this presence, was no living human being, no dweller in our familiar world, not a woman, but a ghost! Oh, it was an awful moment! I pray that I may never again endure another like it. There is something so indescribably frightful in the feeling that we are on the verge of being tried beyond what we can bear, that ordinary conditions are slipping away from under us, that in another moment reason or life itself must snap with the strain; and all these feelings I then underwent. At last I moved, moved backwards from the figure. I dared not attempt to pass her. Yet I could not at first turn away from her. I stepped backwards, facing her still as I did so, till I was close to the fireplace. Then I turned sharply from her, sat down again on the low chair still standing by the hearth, resolutely forcing myself to gaze into the fire, which was blazing cheerfully, though conscious all the time of a terrible fascination urging me to look round again to the middle of the room. Gradually, however, now that I no longer saw her, I began a little to recover myself. I tried to bring my sense and reason to bear on the matter. 'This being,' I said to myself, 'whoever and whatever she is, cannot harm me. I am under God's protection as much at this moment as at any moment of my life. All creatures, even disembodied spirits, if there be such, and this among them, if it be one, are under His control. Why should I be afraid? I am being tried; my courage and trust are being tried to the utmost: let me prove them, let me keep my own self-respect, by mastering this cowardly, unreasonable terror.' And after a time I began to feel stronger and surer of myself. Then I rose from my seat and turned towards the door again; and oh, the relief of seeing that the way was clear; my terrible visitor had disappeared! I hastened across the room, I passed the few steps of passage that lay between my door and the staircase, and hurried down the first flight in a sort of suppressed agony of eagerness to find myself again safe in the living human companionship of my mother and sisters in the cheerful drawing-room below. But my trial was not yet over, indeed it seemed to me afterwards that it had only now reached its height; perhaps the strain on my nervous system was now beginning to tell, and my powers of endurance were all but exhausted. I cannot say if it was so or not. I can only say that my agony of terror, of horror, of absolute fear, was far past describing in words, when, just as I reached the little landing at the foot of the first short staircase, and was on the point of running down the longer flight still before me, I saw again, coming slowly up the steps, as if to meet me, the ghostly figure of the old woman. It was too much. I was reckless by this time; I could not stop. I rushed down the staircase, brushing past the figure as I went: I use the word intentionally—I did brush past her, I felt her. This part of my experience was, I believe, quite at variance with the sensations of orthodox ghost-seers; but I am really telling you all I was conscious of. Then I hardly remember anything more; my agony broke out at last in a loud shrill cry, and I suppose I fainted. I only know that when I recovered my senses I was in the drawing-room, on the sofa, surrounded by my terrified mother and sisters. But it was not for some time that I could find voice or courage to tell them what had happened to me; for several days I was on the brink of a serious illness, and for long afterwards I could not endure to be left alone, even in the broadest daylight."

Lady Farquhar stopped. I fancied, however, from her manner that there was more to tell, so I said nothing; and in a minute or two she went on speaking.

"We did not stay long at Ballyreina after this. I was not sorry to leave it; but still, before the time came for us to do so, I had begun to recover from the most painful part of the impression left upon me by my strange adventure. And when I was at home again, far from the place where it had happened, I gradually lost the feeling of horror altogether, and remembered it only as a very curious and inexplicable experience. Now and then even, I did not shrink from talking about it, generally, I think, with a vague hope that somehow, some time or other, light might be thrown upon it. Not that I ever expected, or could have believed it possible, that the supernatural character of the adventure could be explained away; but I always had a misty fancy that sooner or later I should find out something about my old lady, as we came to call her; who she had been and what her history was."

"And did you?" I asked eagerly.

"Yes, I did," Margaret answered. "To some extent, at least, I learnt the explanation of what I had seen. This was how it was: nearly a year after we had left Ireland I was staying with one of my aunts, and one evening some young people who were also visiting her began to talk about ghosts, and my aunt, who had heard something of the story from my mother, begged me to tell it. I did so, just as I have now told it to you. When I had finished, an elderly lady who was present, and who had listened very attentively, surprised me a little by asking the name of the house where it happened. 'Was it Ballyreina?' she said. I answered 'Yes,' wondering how she knew it, for I had not mentioned it.

"'Then I can tell you whom you saw,' she exclaimed; 'it must have been one of the old Miss Fitzgeralds—the eldest one. The description suits her exactly.'

"I was quite puzzled. We had never heard of any Fitzgeralds at Ballyreina. I said so to the lady, and asked her to explain what she meant. She told me all she knew. It appeared there had been a family of that name for many generations at Ballyreina. Once upon a time—a long-ago once upon a time—the Fitzgeralds had been great and rich; but gradually one misfortune after another had brought them down in the world, and at the time my informant heard about them the only representatives of the old family were three maiden ladies already elderly. Mrs. Gordon, the lady who told me all this, had met them once, and had been much impressed by what she heard of them. They had got poorer and poorer, till at last they had to give up the struggle, and sell, or let on a long lease, their dear old home, Ballyreina. They were too proud to remain in their own country after this, and spent the rest of their lives on the Continent, wandering about from place to place. The most curious part of it was that nearly all their wandering was actually on foot. They were too poor to afford to travel much in the usual way, and yet, once torn from their old associations, the travelling mania seized them; they seemed absolutely unable to rest. So on foot, and speaking not a word of any language but their own, these three desolate sisters journeyed over a great part of the Continent. They visited most of the principal towns, and were well known in several. I daresay they are still remembered at some of the places they used to stay at, though never for more than a short time together. Mrs. Gordon had met them somewhere, I forget where, but it was many years ago. Since then she had never heard of them; she did not know if they were alive or dead; she was only certain that the description of my old lady was exactly like that of the eldest of the sisters, and that the name of their old home was Ballyreina. And I remember her saying, 'If ever a heart was buried in a house, it was that of poor old Miss Fitzgerald.'

"That was all Mrs. Gordon could tell me," continued Lady Farquhar; "but it led to my learning a little more. I told my brother what I had heard. He used often at that time to be in Ireland on business; and to satisfy me, the next time he went he visited the village of Ballyreina again, and in one way and another he found out a few particulars. The house, you remember, had been let to us by a Captain Marchmont. He, my brother discovered, was not the owner of the place, as we had naturally imagined, but only rented it on a very long lease from some ladies of the name of Fitzgerald. It had been in Captain Marchmont's possession for a great many years at the time he let it to us, and the Fitzgeralds, never returning there even to visit it, had come to be almost forgotten. The room with the old-fashioned furniture had been reserved by the owners of the place to leave some of their poor old treasures in—relics too cumbersome to be carried about with them in their strange wanderings, but too precious, evidently, to be parted with. We, of course, never could know what may not have been hidden away in some of the queer old bureaux I told you of. Family papers of importance, perhaps; possibly some ancient love-letters, forgotten in the confusion of their leave-taking; a lock of hair, or a withered flower, perhaps, that she, my poor old lady, would fain have clasped in her hand when dying, or have had buried with her. Ah, yes; there must be many a pitiful old story that is never told."

Lady Farquhar stopped and gazed dreamily and half sadly into the fire.

"Then Miss Fitzgerald was dead when you were at Ballyreina?" I asked.

Margaret looked up with some surprise.

"Did I not say so?" she exclaimed. "That was the point of most interest in what my brother discovered. He could not hear the exact date of her death, but he learnt with certainty that she was dead—had died, at Geneva I think, some time in the month of March in the previous year; the same month, March '55, in which I had twice seen the apparition at Ballyreina."

This was my friend's ghost story.

II

WITNESSED BY TWO

"But to-morrow—to-morrow you will keep for me. I may expect you at the usual time?" said young Mrs. Medway to her old friend Major Graham, as she shook hands with him.

"To-morrow? Certainly. I have kept it for you, Anne. I always said I should," he answered. There was a slight touch of reproach in his tone.

She lifted her eyes for half a second to his face as if she would have said more. But after all it was only the words, "Good-bye, then, till to-morrow," that were uttered, quietly and almost coldly, as Major Graham left the room.

"I can't quite make Anne out sometimes," he said to himself. "She is surely very cold. And yet I know she has real affection for me—sisterly affection, I suppose. Ah, well! so much the better. But still, just when a fellow's off for heaven knows how long, and—and—altogether it does seem a little overstrained. She can't but know what might have come to pass had we not been separated for so long—or had I been richer; and I don't think she could have been exactly in love with Medway, though by all accounts he was a very decent fellow. She is so inconsistent too—she seemed really disappointed when I said I couldn't stay to-day. But I'm a fool to think so much about her. I am as poor as ever and she is rich. A fatal barrier! It's a good thing that she is cold, and that I have plenty of other matters to think about."

And thus congratulating himself he dismissed, or believed that he dismissed for the time being, all thought of Anne Medway from his mind. It was true that he had plenty of other things to occupy it with, for the day after to-morrow was to see his departure from England for an indefinite period.

Mrs. Medway meantime sat sadly and silently in the library where Major Graham had left her. Her sweet gray eyes were fixed on the fire burning brightly and cheerfully in the waning afternoon light, but she saw nothing about her. Her thoughts were busily travelling along a road which had grown very familiar to them of late: she was recalling all her past intercourse with Kenneth Graham since the time when, as boy and girl, they had scarcely remembered that they were not "real" brother and sister—all through the pleasant years of frequent meeting and unconstrained companionship to the melancholy day when Kenneth was ordered to India, and they bade each other a long farewell! That was ten years ago now, and they had not met again till last spring, when Major Graham returned to find his old playfellow a widow, young, rich, and lovely, but lonely in a sense—save that she had two children—for she was without near relations, and was not the type of woman to make quick or numerous friendships.

The renewal of the old relations had been very pleasant—only too pleasant, Anne had of late begun to think. For the news of Kenneth's having decided to go abroad again had made her realise all he had become to her, and the discovery brought with it sharp misgiving, and even humiliation.

"He does not care for me—not as I do for him," she was saying to herself as she sat by the fire. "There would have been no necessity for his leaving England again had he done so. It cannot be because I am rich and he poor, surely? He is not the sort of man to let such a mere accident as that stand in the way if he really cared for me. No, it is that he does not care for me except as a sort of sister. But still—he said he had kept his last evening for me—at least he cares for no one else more, and that is something. Who knows—perhaps to-morrow—when it comes to really saying good-bye—?" and a faint flush of renewed hope rose to her cheeks and a brighter gleam to her eyes.

The door opened, and a gray-haired man-servant came in gently.

"I beg your pardon, ma'am," he said apologetically; "I was not sure if Major Graham had gone. Will he be here to dinner, if you please?"

"Not to-night, Ambrose. I shall be quite alone. But Major Graham will dine here to-morrow; he does not leave till Thursday morning."

"Very well, ma'am," said Ambrose, as he discreetly retired.

He had been many years in the Medway household. He had respected his late master, but for his young mistress he had actual affection, and being of a somewhat sentimental turn, he had constructed for her benefit a very pretty little romance of which Major Graham was the hero. It had been a real blow to poor Ambrose to learn that the gentleman in question was on the eve of his departure without any sign of a satisfactory third volume, and he was rather surprised to see that Mrs. Medway seemed this evening in better spirits than for some time past.

"It's maybe understood between themselves," he reflected, as he made his way back to his own quarters. "I'm sure I hope so, for he's a real gentleman and she's as sweet a lady as ever stepped, which I should know if any one should, having seen her patience with poor master as was really called for through his long illness. She deserves a happy ending, and I'm sure I hope she may have it, poor lady."

"To-morrow at the usual time," meaning five o'clock or thereabouts, brought Kenneth for his last visit. Anne had been expecting him with an anxiety she was almost ashamed to own to herself, yet her manner was so calm and collected that no one could have guessed the tumult of hope and fear, of wild grief at his leaving, of intense longing for any word—were it but a word—to prove that all was not on her side only.

"I could bear his being away—for years even, if he thought it must be—if I could but look forward—if I had the right to look forward to his return," she said to herself.

But the evening passed on tranquilly, and to all appearance pleasantly, without a word or look more than might have been between real brother and sister. Kenneth talked kindly—tenderly even—of the past; repeated more than once the pleasure it had been to him to find again his old friend so little changed, so completely his old friend still. The boys came in to say good-night, and "good-bye, alas! my lads," added their tall friend with a sigh. "Don't forget me quite, Hal and Charlie, and don't let your mother forget me either, eh?" To which the little fellows replied solemnly, though hardly understanding why he patted their curly heads with a lingering hand this evening, or why mamma looked grave at his words.

And Anne bore it all without flinching, and smiled and talked a little more than usual perhaps, though all the time her heart was bursting, and Kenneth wondered more than ever if, after all, she had "much heart or feeling to speak of."

"You will be bringing back a wife with you perhaps," she said once. "Shall you tell her about your sister Anne, Kenneth?"

Major Graham looked at her earnestly for half an instant before he replied, but Anne's eyes were not turned towards him, and she did not see the look. And his words almost belied it.

"Certainly I shall tell her of you," he said, "that is to say, if she ever comes to exist. At present few things are less probable. Still I am old enough now never to say, 'Fontaine, je ne boirai jamais de ton eau.' But," he went on, "I may return to find you married again, Anne. You are still so young and you are rather lonely."

"No," said Anne with a sudden fierceness which he had never seen in her before, "I shall never marry again—never," and she looked him full in the face with a strange sparkle in her eyes which almost frightened him.

"I beg your pardon," he said meekly. And though the momentary excitement faded as quickly as it had come, and Anne, murmuring some half-intelligible excuse, was again her quiet self, this momentary glimpse of a fierier nature beneath gave him food for reflection.

"Can Medway have not been what he seemed on the surface, after all?" he thought to himself. "What can make her so vindictive against matrimony?"

But it was growing late, and Kenneth had still some last preparations to make. He rose slowly and reluctantly from his chair.

"I must be going, I fear," he said.

Anne too had risen. They stood together on the hearthrug. A slight, very slight shiver passed through her. Kenneth perceived it.

"You have caught cold, I fear," he said kindly; for the room was warm and the fire was burning brightly.

"No, I don't think so," she said indifferently.

"You will write to me now and then?" he said next.

"Oh, certainly—not very often perhaps," she replied lightly, "but now and then. Stay," and she turned away towards her writing-table, "tell me exactly how to address you. Your name—is your surname enough?—there is no other Graham in your regiment?"

"No," he said absently, "I suppose not. Yes, just my name and the regiment and Allagherry, which will be our headquarters. You might, if you were very amiable—you might write to Galles—a letter overland would wait for me there," for it was the days of "long sea" for all troops to India.

Anne returned to her former position on the hearthrug—the moment at the table had restored her courage. "We shall see," she said, smiling again.

Then Kenneth said once more, "I must go;" but he lingered still a moment.

"You must have caught cold, Anne, or else you are very tired. You are so white," and from his height above her, though Anne herself was tall, he laid his hand on her shoulder gently and as a brother might have done, and looked down at her pale face half inquiringly. A flush of colour rose for an instant to her cheeks. The temptation was strong upon her to throw off that calmly caressing hand, but she resisted it, and looked up bravely with a light almost of defiance in her eyes.

"I am perfectly well, I assure you. But perhaps I am a little tired. I suppose it is getting late."

And Kenneth stifled a sigh of scarcely realised disappointment, and quickly drew back his hand.

"Yes, it is late. I am very thoughtless. Good-bye then, Anne. God bless you."

And before she had time to answer he was gone.

Ambrose met him in the hall, with well-meaning officiousness bringing forward his coat and hat. His presence helped to dissipate an impulse which seized Major Graham to rush upstairs again for one other word of farewell. Had he done so what would he have found? Anne sobbing—sobbing with the terrible intensity of a self-contained nature once the strain is withdrawn—sobbing in the bitterness of her grief and the cruelty of her mortification, with but one consolation.

"At least he does not despise me. I hid it well," she whispered to herself.

And Kenneth Graham, as he drove away in his cab, repeated to himself, "She is so cold, this evening particularly. And yet, can it be that it was to hide any other feeling? If I thought so—good God!" and he half started up as if to call to the driver, but sat down again. "No, no, I must not be a fool. I could not stand a repulse from her—I could never see her again. Better not risk it. And then I am so poor!"

And in the bustle and hurry of his departure he tried to forget the wild fancy which for a moment had disturbed him. He sailed the next day.

But the few weeks which followed passed heavily for Anne. It was a dead time of year—there was no special necessity for her exerting herself to throw off the overwhelming depression, and strong and brave as she was, she allowed herself, to some extent, to yield to it.

"If only he had not come back—if I had never seen him again!" she repeated to herself incessantly. "I had in a sense forgotten him—the thought of him never troubled me all the years of my marriage. I suppose I had never before understood how I could care. How I wish I had never learnt it! How I wish he had never come back!"

It was above all in the afternoons—the dull, early dark, autumn afternoons—which for some weeks had been enlivened by the expectation, sure two or three times a week to be fulfilled, of Major Graham's "dropping in"—that the aching pain, the weary longing, grew so bad as to be well-nigh intolerable.

"How shall I bear it?" said poor Anne to herself sometimes; "it is so wrong, so unwomanly! So selfish, too, when I think of my children. How much I have to be thankful for—why should I ruin my life by crying for the one thing that is not for me? It is worse, far worse than if he had died; had I known that he had loved me, I could have borne his death, it seems to me."

She was sitting alone one afternoon about five weeks after Kenneth had left, thinking sadly over and over the same thoughts, when a tap at the door made her look up.

"Come in," she said, though the tap hardly sounded like that of her maid, and no one else was likely to come to the door of her own room where she happened to be. "Come in," and somewhat to her surprise the door half opened and old Ambrose's voice replied—

"If you please, ma'am—" then stopped and hesitated.

"Come in," she repeated with a touch of impatience. "What is it, Ambrose? Where is Seton?"

"If you please, ma'am, I couldn't find her—that is to say," Ambrose went on nervously, "I didn't look for her. I thought, ma'am, I would rather tell you myself. You mustn't be startled, ma'am," and Anne at this looking up at the old man saw that he was pale and startled-looking himself, "but it's—it's Major Graham."

"Major Graham?" repeated Anne, and to herself her voice sounded almost like a scream. "What about him? Have you heard anything?"

"It's him, ma'am—him himself!" said Ambrose. "He's in the library. I'm a little afraid, ma'am, there may be something wrong—he looked so strange and he did not answer when I spoke to him. But he's in the library, ma'am."

Anne did not wait to hear more. She rushed past Ambrose, across the landing, and down the two flights of steps which led to the library—a half-way house room, between the ground-floor and the drawing-room—almost before his voice had stopped. At the door she hesitated a moment, and in that moment all sorts of wild suppositions flashed across her brain. What was it? What was she going to hear? Had Kenneth turned back half-way out to India for her sake? Had some trouble befallen him, in which he had come to seek her sympathy? What could it be? and her heart beating so as almost to suffocate her, she opened the door.

Yes—there he stood—on the hearthrug as she had last seen him in that room. But he did not seem to hear her come in, for he made no movement towards her; he did not even turn his head in her direction.

More and more startled and perturbed, Anne hastily went up to him.

"Kenneth," she cried, "what is it? What is the matter?"

She had held out her hand as she hurried towards him, but he did not seem to see it. He stood there still, without moving—his face slightly turned away, till she was close beside him.

"Kenneth," she repeated, this time with a thrill of something very like anguish in her tone, "what is the matter? Are you angry with me? Kenneth—speak."

Then at last he slowly turned his head and looked at her with a strange, half-wistful anxiety in his eyes—he gazed at her as if his very soul were in that gaze, and lifting his right hand, gently laid it on her shoulder as he had done the evening he had bidden her farewell. She did not shrink from his touch, but strange to say, she did not feel it, and some indefinable instinct made her turn her eyes away from his and glance at her shoulder. But even as she did so she saw that his hand was no longer there, and with a thrill of fear she exclaimed again, "Speak, Kenneth, speak to me!"

The words fell on empty air. There was no Kenneth beside her. She was standing on the hearthrug alone.

Then, for the first time, there came over her that awful chill of terror so often described, yet so indescribable to all but the few who have felt it for themselves. With a terrible though half-stifled cry, Anne turned towards the door. It opened before she reached it, and she half fell into old Ambrose's arms. Fortunately for her—for her reason, perhaps—his vague misgiving had made him follow her, though of what he was afraid he could scarcely have told.

"Oh, ma'am—oh, my poor lady!" he exclaimed, as he half led, half carried her back to her own room, "what is it? Has he gone? But how could he have gone? I was close by—I never saw him pass."

"He is not there—he has not been there," said poor Anne, trembling and clinging to her old servant. "Oh, Ambrose, what you and I have seen was no living Kenneth Graham—no living man at all. Ambrose—he came thus to say good-bye to me. He is dead," and the tears burst forth as she spoke, and Anne sobbed convulsively.

Ambrose looked at her in distress and consternation past words. Then at last he found courage to speak.

"My poor lady," he repeated. "It must be so. I misdoubted me and I did not know why. He did not ring, but I was passing by the door and something—a sort of feeling that there was some one waiting outside—made me open it. To my astonishment it was he," and Ambrose himself could not repress a sort of tremor. "He did not speak, but seemed to pass me and be up the stairs and in the library in an instant. And then, not knowing what to do, I went to your room, ma'am. Forgive me if I did wrong."

"No, no," said Anne, "you could not have done otherwise. Ring the bell, Ambrose; tell Seton I have had bad news, and that you think it has upset me. But wait at the door till she comes. I—I am afraid to be left alone."

And Mrs. Medway looked so deadly pale and faint, that when Seton came hurrying in answer to the sharply-rung bell, it needed no explanation for her to see that Mrs. Medway was really ill. Seton was a practical, matter-of-fact person, and the bustle of attending to her mistress, trying to make her warm again—for Anne was shivering with cold—and persuading her to take some restoratives, effectually drove any inquiry as to the cause of the sudden seizure out of the maid's head. And by the time Mrs. Medway was better, Seton had invented a satisfactory explanation of it all, for herself.

"You need a change, ma'am. It's too dull for anybody staying in town at this season; and it's beginning to tell on your nerves, ma'am," was the maid's idea.

And some little time after the strange occurrence Mrs. Medway was persuaded to leave town for the country.

But not till she had seen in the newspapers the fatal paragraph she knew would sooner or later be there—the announcement of the death, on board Her Majesty's troopship Ariadne a few days before reaching the Cape, of "Major R. R. Graham," of the 113th regiment.

She "had known it," she said to herself; yet when she saw it there, staring her in the face, she realised that she had been living in a hope which she had not allowed to herself that the apparition might in the end prove capable of other explanation. She would gladly have taken refuge in the thought that it was a dream, an optical delusion fed of her fancy incessantly brooding on her friend and on his last visit—that her brain was in some way disarranged or disturbed—anything, anything would have been welcome to her. But against all such was opposed the fact that it was not herself alone who had seen Kenneth Graham that fatal afternoon.

And now, when the worst was certain, she recognised this still more clearly as the strongest testimony to the apparition not having been the product of her own imagination. And old Ambrose, her sole confidant, in his simple way agreed with her.

"If I had not seen him too, ma'am, or if I alone had seen him," he said, furtively wiping his eyes. "But the two of us. No, it could have but the one meaning," and he looked sadly at the open newspaper. "There's a slight discrimpancy, ma'am," he said as he pointed to the paragraph. "Our Major Graham's name was 'K. R.' not 'R. R.'"

"It is only a misprint. I noticed that," said Anne wearily. "No, Ambrose, there can be no mistake. But I do not want any one—not any one—ever to hear the story. You will promise me that, Ambrose?" and the old man repeated the promise he had already given.

There was another "discrimpancy" which had struck Anne more forcibly, but which she refrained from mentioning to Ambrose.

"It can mean nothing; it is no use putting it into his head," she said to herself. "Still, it is strange."

The facts were these. The newspaper gave the date of Major Graham's death as the 25th November—the afternoon on which he had appeared to Mrs. Medway and her servant was that of the 26th. This left no possibility of calculating that the vision had occurred at or even shortly after the moment of the death.

"It must be a mistake in the announcement," Anne decided. And then she gave herself up to the acceptance of the fact. Kenneth was dead. Life held no individual future for her any more—nothing to look forward to, no hopes, however tremblingly admitted, that "some day" he might return, and return to discover—to own, perhaps, to himself and to her that he did love her, and that only mistaken pride, or her own coldness, or one of the hundred "mistakes" or "perhapses" by which men, so much more than women, allow to drift away from them the happiness they might grasp, had misled and withheld him! No; all was over. Henceforth she must live in her children alone—in the interests of others she must find her happiness.

"And in one blessed thought," said the poor girl—for she was little more—even at the first to herself; "that after all he did love me, that I may, without shame, say so in my heart, for I was his last thought. It was—it must have been—to tell me so that he came that day. My Kenneth—yes, he was mine after all."

Some little time passed. In the quiet country place whither, sorely against Seton's desires, Mrs. Medway had betaken herself for "change," she heard no mention of Major Graham's death. One or two friends casually alluded to it in their letters as "very sad," but that was all. And Anne was glad of it.

"I must brace myself to hear it spoken of and discussed by the friends who knew him well—who knew how well I knew him"—she reflected. "But I am glad to escape it for a while."

It was February already, more than three months since Kenneth Graham had left England, when one morning—among letters forwarded from her London address—came a thin foreign paper one with the traces of travel upon it—of which the superscription made Anne start and then turn pale and cold.

"I did not think of this," she said to herself. "He must have left it to be forwarded to me. It is terrible—getting a letter after the hand that wrote it has been long dead and cold."

With trembling fingers she opened it.

"My dear—may I say my dearest Anne," were the first words that her eyes fell on. Her own filled with tears. Wiping them away before going on to read more, she caught sight of the date. "On board H.M.'s troopship Ariadne, 27th November."

Anne started. Stranger and stranger. Two days later than the reported date of his death—and the writing so strong and clear. No sign of weakness or illness even! She read on with frantic eagerness; it was not a very long letter, but when Anne had read the two or three somewhat hurriedly written pages, her face had changed as if from careworn, pallid middle age, back to fresh, sunny youth. She fell on her knees in fervent, unspoken thanksgiving. She kissed the letter—the dear, beautiful letter, as if it were a living thing!

"It is too much—too much," she said. "What have I done to deserve such blessedness?"

This was what the letter told. The officer whose death had been announced was not "our Major Graham," not Graham of the 113th at all, but an officer belonging to another regiment who had come on board at Madeira to return to India, believing his health to be quite restored. "The doctors had in some way mistaken his case," wrote Kenneth, "for he broke down again quite suddenly and died two days ago. He was a very good fellow, and we have all been very cut up about it. He took a fancy to me, and I have been up some nights with him, and I am rather done up myself. I write this to post at the Cape, for a fear has struck me that—his initials being so like mine—some report may reach you that it is I, not he. Would you care very much, dear Anne? I dare to think you would—but I cannot in a letter tell you why. I must wait till I see you. I have had a somewhat strange experience, and it is possible, just possible, that I may be able to tell you all about it, vivâ voce, sooner than I had any idea of when I last saw you. In the meantime, good-bye and God bless you, my dear child."

Then followed a postscript—of some days' later date, written in great perturbation of spirit at finding that the letter had, by mistake, not been posted at the Cape. "After all my anxiety that you should see it as soon as or before the newspapers, it is really too bad. I cannot understand how it happened. I suppose it was that I was so busy getting poor Graham's papers and things together to send on shore, that I overlooked it. It cannot now be posted till we get to Galles."

That was all. But was it not enough, and more than enough? The next few weeks passed for Anne Medway like a happy dream. She was content now to wait—years even—she had recovered faith in herself, faith in the future.

The next Indian mail brought her no letter, somewhat to her surprise. She wondered what had made Kenneth allude to his perhaps seeing her again before long—she wondered almost more, what was the "strange experience" to which he referred. Could it have had any connection with her most strange experience that November afternoon? And thus "wondering" she was sitting alone—in her own house again by this time—one evening towards the end of April, when a ring at the bell made her look up from the book she was reading, half dreamily asking herself what visitor could be coming so late. She heard steps and voices—a door shutting—then Ambrose opened that of the drawing-room where she was sitting and came up to her, his wrinkled old face all flushed and beaming.

"It was me that frightened you so that day, ma'am," he began. "It's right it should be me again. But it's himself—his very own self this time. You may believe me, indeed."

Anne started to her feet. She felt herself growing pale—she trembled so that she could scarcely stand.

"Where is he?" she said. "You have not put him into the library—anywhere but there?"

"He would have it so, ma'am. He said he would explain to you. Oh, go to him, ma'am—you'll see it'll be all right."

Anne made her way to the library. But at the door a strange tremor seized her. She could scarcely control herself to open it. Yes—there again on the hearthrug stood the tall figure she had so often pictured thus to herself. She trembled and all but fell, but his voice—his own hearty, living voice—speaking to her in accents tenderer and deeper than ever heretofore—reassured her, and dispersed at once the fear that had hovered about her.

"Anne, my dear Anne. It is I myself. Don't look so frightened;" and in a moment he had led her forward, and stood with his hand on her shoulder, looking with his kind, earnest eyes into hers.

"Yes," he said dreamily, "it was just thus. Oh, how often I have thought of this moment! Anne, if I am mistaken forgive my presumption, but I can't think I am. Anne, my darling, you do love me?"

There was no need of words. Anne hid her face on his shoulder for one happy moment. Then amidst the tears that would come she told him all—all she had suffered and hoped and feared—her love and her agony of humiliation when she thought it was not returned—her terrible grief when she thought him dead; and yet the consolation of believing herself to have been his last thought in life.

"So you shall be—my first and my last," he answered. "My Anne—my very own."

And then she told him more of the strange story we know. He listened with intense eagerness, but without testifying much surprise, far less incredulity.

"I anticipated something of the kind," he said, after a moment or two of silence. "It is very strange. Listen, Anne: at the time, the exact time, so far as I can roughly calculate, at which you thought you saw me, I was dreaming of you. It was between four and five o'clock in the afternoon, was it not?"

Anne bowed her head in assent.

"That would have made it about six o'clock where we then were," he went on consideringly. "Yes; it was about seven when I awoke. I had lain down that afternoon with a frightful headache. Poor Graham had died shortly before midnight the night before, and I had not been able to sleep, though I was very tired. I daresay I was not altogether in what the doctors call a normal condition, from the physical fatigue and the effect generally of having watched him die. I was feeling less earthly, if you can understand, than one usually does. It is—to me at least—impossible to watch a deathbed without wondering about it all—about what comes after—intensely. And Graham was so good, so patient and resigned and trustful, though it was awfully hard for him to die. He had every reason to wish to live. Well, Anne, when I fell asleep that afternoon I at once began dreaming about you. I had been thinking about you a great deal, constantly almost, ever since we set sail. For, just before starting, I had got a hint that this appointment—I have not told you about it yet, but that will keep; I have accepted it, as you see by my being here—I got a hint that it would probably be offered me, and that if I didn't mind paying my passage back almost as soon as I got out, I had better make up my mind to accept it. I felt that it hung upon you, and yet I did not see how to find out what you would say without—without risking what I had—your sisterly friendship. It came into my head just as I was falling asleep that I would write to you from the Cape, and tell you of Graham's death to avoid any mistaken report, and that I might in my letter somehow feel my way a little. This was all in my mind, and as I fell asleep it got confused so that I did not know afterwards clearly where to separate it from my dream."

"And what was the dream?" asked Anne breathlessly.

"Almost precisely what you saw," he replied. "I fancied myself here—rushing upstairs to the library in my haste to see you—to tell you I was not dead, and to ask you if you would have cared much had it been so. I saw all the scene—the hall, the staircase already lighted. This room—and you coming in at the door with a half-frightened, half-eager look in your face. Then it grew confused. I next remember standing here beside you on the hearthrug with my hand on your shoulder—thus, Anne—and gazing into your eyes, and struggling, struggling to ask you what I wanted so terribly to know. But the words would not come, and the agony seemed to awake me. Yet with the awaking came the answer. Something had answered me; I said to myself, 'Yes, Anne does love me.'"

And Anne remembered the strange feeling of joy which had come to her even in the first bitterness of her grief. She turned to the hand that still lay on her shoulder and kissed it. "Oh, Kenneth," she said, "how thankful we should be! But how strange, to think that we owe all to a dream! Was it a dream, Kenneth?"

He shook his head.

"You must ask that of wiser people than I," he said. "I suppose it was."

"But how could it have been a dream?" said Anne again. "You forget, Kenneth—Ambrose saw you too."

"Though I did not see him, nor even think of him. Yes, that makes it even more incomprehensible. It must have been the old fellow's devotion to you, Anne, that made him sympathise with you, somehow."

"I am glad he saw you," said Anne. "I should prefer to think it more than a dream. And there is always more evidence in favour of any story of the kind if it has been witnessed by two. But there is one other thing I want to ask you. It has struck me since that you answered me rather abstractedly that last evening when I spoke about your address, and asked if there was any other of the name in your regiment. Once or twice I have drawn a faint ray of hope from remembering your not very decided answer."

"Yes, it was stupid of me; I half remembered it afterwards. I should have explained it, but it scarcely seemed worth while. I did know another Major Graham might be joining us at Funchal, for that very day I had been entrusted with letters for him. But I was abstracted that evening, Anne. I was trying to persuade myself I didn't care for what I now know I care for more than for life itself—your love—Anne."

III

UNEXPLAINED

PART I

"For facts are stubborn things."—Smollett.

"Silberbach! What in the name of everything that is eccentric should you go there for? The most uninteresting, out-of-the-way, altogether unattractive little hole in all Germany? What can have put Silberbach in your head?"

"I really don't know," I answered, rather tired, to tell the truth, of the discussion. "There doesn't seem any particular reason why anybody ever should go to Silberbach, except that Goethe and the Duke of Weimar are supposed to have gone there to dance with the peasant maidens. I certainly don't see that that is any reason why I should go there. Still, on the other hand, I don't see that it is any reason why I should not? I only want to find some thoroughly country place where the children and I can do as we like for a fortnight or so. It is really too hot to stay in a town, even a little town like this."

"Yes, that is true," said my friend. "It is a pity you took up your quarters in the town. You might have taken a little villa outside, and then you would not have needed to go away at all."

"I wanted a rest from housekeeping, and our queer old inn is very comfortable," I said. "Besides, being here, would it not be a pity to go away without seeing anything of the far-famed Thuringian Forest?"

"Yes, certainly it would. I quite agree with you about everything except about Silberbach. That is what I cannot get over. You have not enough self-assertion, my dear. I am certain Silberbach is some freak of Herr von Walden's—most unpractical man. Why, I really am not at all sure that you will get anything to eat there."

"I am not afraid of that part of it," I replied philosophically. "With plenty of milk, fresh eggs, and bread and butter, we can always get on. And those I suppose we are sure to find."

"Milk and eggs—yes, I suppose so. Butter is doubtful once you leave the tourist track, and the bread will be the sour bread of the country."

"I don't mind that—nor do the children. But if the worst comes to the worst we need not stay at Silberbach—we can always get away."

"That is certainly true; if one can get there, one can, I suppose, always get away," answered Fräulein Ottilia with a smile, "though I confess it is a curious inducement to name for going to a place—that one can get away from it! However, we need not say any more about it. I see your heart is set on Silberbach, and I am quite sure I shall have the satisfaction of hearing you own I was right in trying to dissuade you from it, when you come back again," she added, rather maliciously.

"Perhaps so. But it is not only Silberbach we are going to. We shall see lots of other places. Herr von Walden has planned it all. The first three days we shall travel mostly on foot. I think it will be great fun. Nora and Reggie are enchanted. Of course I would not travel on foot alone with them; it would hardly be safe, I suppose?"

"Safe? oh yes, safe enough. The peasants are very quiet, civil people—honest and kindly, though generally desperately poor! But you would be safe enough anywhere in Thuringia. It is not like Alsace, where now and then one does meet with rather queer customers in the forests. So good-bye, then, my dear, for the next two or three weeks—and may you enjoy yourself."

"Especially at Silberbach?"

"Even at Silberbach—that is to say, even if I have to own you were right and I wrong. Yes, my dear, I am unselfish enough to hope you will return having found Silberbach an earthly paradise."

And waving her hand in adieu, kind Fräulein Ottilia stood at her garden-gate watching me make my way down the dusty road.

"She is a little prejudiced, I daresay," I thought to myself. "Prejudiced against Herr von Walden's choice, for I notice every one here has their pet places and their special aversions. I daresay we shall like Silberbach, and if not, we need not stay there after the Waldens leave us. Anyway, I shall be thankful to get out of this heat into the real country."

I was spending the summer in a part of Germany hitherto new ground to me. We had—the "we" meaning myself and my two younger children, Nora of twelve and Reggie of nine—settled down for the greater part of the time in a small town on the borders of the Thuringian Forest. Small, but not in its own estimation unimportant, for it was a "Residenz," with a fortress of sufficiently ancient date to be well worth visiting, even had the view from its ramparts been far less beautiful than it was. And had the little town possessed no attractions of its own, natural or artificial, the extreme cordiality and kindness of its most hospitable inhabitants would have left the pleasantest impression on my mind. I was sorry to leave my friends even for two or three weeks, but it was too hot! Nora was pale and Reggie's noble appetite gave signs of flagging. Besides—as I had said to Ottilia—it would be too absurd to have come so far and not see the lions of the neighbourhood.

So we were to start the next morning for an excursion in the so-called "Forest," in the company of Herr von Walden, his wife and son, and two young men, friends of the latter. We were to travel by rail over the first part of the ground, uninteresting enough, till we reached a point where we could make our way on foot through the woods for a considerable distance. Then, after spending the night in a village whose beautiful situation had tempted some enterprising speculator to build a good hotel, we proposed the next day to plunge still deeper into the real recesses of the forest, walking and driving by turns, in accordance with our inclination and the resources of the country in respect of Einspänners—the light carriage with the horse invariably yoked at one side of the pole instead of between shafts, in which one gets about more speedily and safely than might be imagined. And at the end of three or four days of this, weather permitting, agreeably nomad life, our friends the Waldens, obliged to return to their home in the town from which we started, were to leave my children and me for a fortnight's country air in this same village of Silberbach which Ottilia so vehemently objected to. I did not then, I do not now, know— and I am pretty sure he himself could not say—why our guide, Herr von Walden, had chosen Silberbach from among the dozens of other villages which could quite as well—as events proved, indeed, infinitely better—have served our very simple purpose. It was a chance, as such things often are, but a chance which, as you will see, left its mark in a manner which can never be altogether effaced from my memory.

The programme was successfully carried out. The weather was magnificent. Nobody fell ill or footsore, or turned out unexpectedly bad-tempered. And it was hot enough, even in the forest shades, which we kept to as much as possible, to have excused some amount of irritability. But we were all sound and strong, and had entered into a tacit compact of making the best of things and enjoying ourselves as much as we could. Nora and Reggie perhaps, by the end of the second day, began to have doubts as to the delights of indefinitely continued walking excursions; and though they would not have owned to it, they were not, I think, sorry to hear that the greater part of the fourth day's travels was to be on wheels. But they were very well off. Lutz von Walden and his two friends—a young baron, rather the typical "German student" in appearance, though in reality as hearty and unsentimental as any John Bull of his age and rank—and George Norman, an English boy of seventeen or eighteen, "getting up" German for an army examination—were all three only too ready to carry my little boy on their backs on any sign of over-fatigue. And, indeed, more than one hint reached me that they would willingly have done the same by Nora, had the dignity of her twelve years allowed of such a thing. She scarcely looked her age at that time, but she was very conscious of having entered "on her teens," and the struggle between this new importance and her hitherto almost boyish tastes was amusing to watch. She was strong and healthy in the extreme, intelligent though not precocious, observant but rather matter-of-fact, with no undue development of the imagination, nothing that by any kind of misapprehension or exaggeration could have been called "morbid" about her. It was a legend in the family that the word "nerves" existed not for Nora: she did not know the meaning of fear, physical or moral. I could sometimes wish she had never learnt otherwise. But we must take the bad with the good, the shadow inseparable from the light. The first perception of things not dreamt of in her simple childish philosophy came to Nora as I would not have chosen it; but so, I must believe, it had to be.

"Where are we to sleep to-night, Herr von Walden, please?" asked Reggie from the heights of Lutz's broad shoulders, late that third afternoon, when we were all, not the children only, beginning to think that a rest even in the barest of inn parlours, and a dinner even of the most modest description, would be very welcome.

"Don't tease so, Reggie," said Nora. "I'm sure Herr von Walden has told you the name twenty times already."

"Yes, but I forget it," urged the child; and good-natured Herr von Walden, nowise loath to do so again, took up the tale of our projected doings and destinations.

"To-night, my dear child, we sleep at the pretty little town—yes, town I may almost call it—of Seeberg. It stands in what I may call an oasis of the forest, which stops abruptly, and begins again some miles beyond Seeberg. We should be there in another hour or so," he went on, consulting his watch. "I have, of course, written for rooms there, as I have done to all the places where we mean to halt. And so far I have not proved a bad courier, I flatter myself?"

He paused, and looked round him complacently.

"No, indeed," replied everybody. "The very contrary. We have got on capitally."

At which the beaming face of our commander-in-chief beamed still more graciously.

"And to-morrow," continued Reggie in his funny German, pounding away vigorously at Lutz's shoulders meanwhile, "what do we do to-morrow? We must have an Einspänner—is it not so? not that we are tired, but you said we had far to go."

"Yes, an Einspänner for the ladies—your amiable mother, Miss Nora, and my wife, and you, Reggie, will find a corner beside the driver. Myself and these young fellows," indicating the three friends by a wave of the hand, "will start from Seeberg betimes, giving you rendez vous at Ulrichsthal, where there are some famous ruins. And you must not forget," he added, turning to his wife and me, "to stop at Grünstein as you pass, and spend a quarter of an hour in the china manufactory there."

"Just what I wanted," said Frau von Walden. "I have a tea-service from there, and I am in hopes of matching it. I had a good many breakages last winter with a dreadfully careless servant, and there is a good deal to replace."

"I don't think I know the Grünstein china," I said. "Is it very pretty?"

"It is very like the blue-and-white that one sees so much of with us," said Frau von Walden. "That, the ordinary blue-and-white, is made at Blauenstein. But there is more variety of colours at Grünstein. They are rather more enterprising there, I fancy, and perhaps there is a finer quality of china clay, or whatever they call it, in that neighbourhood. I often wonder the Thuringian china is not more used in England, where you are so fond of novelties."

"And where nothing is so appreciated as what comes from a distance," said George Norman. "By Jove! isn't that a pretty picture!" he broke off suddenly, and we all stood still to admire.

It was the month of August; already the subdued evening lights were replacing the brilliant sunshine and blue sky of the glowing summer day. We were in the forest, through which at this part ran the main road which we were following to Seeberg. At one side of the road the ground descended abruptly to a considerable depth, and there in the defile far beneath us ran a stream, on one bank of which the trees had been for some distance cleared away, leaving a strip of pasture of the most vivid green imaginable. And just below where we stood, a goatherd, in what—thanks possibly to the enchantment of the distance—appeared a picturesque costume, was slowly making his way along, piping as he went, and his flock, of some fifteen or twenty goats of every colour and size, following him according to their own eccentric fashion, some scrambling on the bits of rock a little way up the ascending ground, others quietly browsing here and there on their way—the tinkling of their collar-bells reaching us with a far-away, silvery sound through the still softer and fainter notes of the pipe. There was something strangely fascinating about it all—something pathetic in the goatherd's music, simple, barbaric even as it was, and in the distant, uncertain tinkling, which impressed us all, and for a moment or two no one spoke.

"What is it that it reminds me of?" said Lutz suddenly. "I seem to have seen and heard it all before."

"Yes, I know exactly how you mean," I replied. "It is like a dream;" and as I said so, I walked on again a little in advance of the others with Lutz and his rider. For I thought I saw a philosophical or metaphysical dissertation preparing in Herr von Walden's bent brows and general look of absorption, and somehow, just then, it would have spoilt it all. Lutz seemed instinctively to understand, for he too for a moment or so was silent, when suddenly a joyful cry arose.

"Seeberg!" exclaimed several voices; for the first sight of our temporary destination broke upon the view all at once, as is often the case in these more or less wooded districts. One travels for hours together as if in an enchanted land of changeless monotony; trees, trees everywhere and nothing but trees—one could fancy late in the afternoon that one was back at the early morning's starting-point—when suddenly the forest stops, sharply and completely, where the hand of man has decreed that it should, not by gradual degrees as when things have been left to the gentler management of nature and time.

So our satisfaction was the greater from not having known the goal of that day's journey to be so near. We began to allow to each other for the first time that we were "a little tired," and with far less hesitation that we were "very hungry." Still we were not a very dilapidated-looking party when the inhabitants of Seeberg turned out at doors and windows to inspect us. Reggie, of course, whom no consideration could induce to make his entry on Lutz's shoulders, looking the freshest of all, and eliciting many complimentary remarks from the matrons and maidens of the place as we passed.

Our quarters at Seeberg met with the approval of everybody. The supper was excellent, our rooms as clean and comfortable as could be wished.

"So far," I could not help saying to my friends, "I have seen no signs of the 'roughing it' for which you prepared me. I call this luxurious."

"Yes, this is very comfortable," said Herr von Walden. "At Silberbach, which we shall reach to-morrow evening, all will be much more homely."

"But that is what I like," I maintained stoutly. "I assure you I am not at all difficile, as the French say."

"Still," began Frau von Walden, "are you sure that you know what 'roughing it' means? One has such romantic, unpractical ideas till one really tries it. For me, I confess, there is something very depressing in being without all the hundred and one little comforts, not to say luxuries, that have become second nature to us, and yet I do not think I am a self-indulgent woman."

"Certainly not," I said, and with sincerity.

"If it were necessary," she went on, "I hope I should be quite ready to live in a cottage and make the best of it cheerfully. But when it is not necessary? Don't you think, my dear friend, it would perhaps be wiser for you to arrange to spend your two or three weeks here, and not go on to Silberbach? You might return here to-morrow from Ulrichsthal while we make our way home, by Silberbach, if my husband really wishes to see it."

I looked at her in some surprise. What possessed everybody to caution me so against Silberbach? Everybody, that is to say, except Herr von Walden himself. A spice of contradiction began to influence me. Perhaps the worthy Herr had himself been influenced in the same way more than he realised.

"I don't see why I should do so," I said. "We expect really to enjoy ourselves at Silberbach. You have no reason for advising me to give it up?"

"No, oh no—none in particular," she replied. "I have only a feeling that it is rather out of the way and lonely for you. Supposing, for instance, one of the children got ill there?"

"Oh, my dear, you are too fanciful," said her husband. "Why should the children get ill there more than anywhere else? If one thought of all these possibilities one would never stir from home."

"And you know my maid is ready to follow me as soon as I quite settle where we shall stay," I said. "I shall not be alone more than four-and-twenty hours. Of course it would have been nonsense to bring Lina with us; she would have been quite out of her element during our walking expeditions."

"And I have a very civil note from the inn at Silberbach, the 'Katze,'" said Herr von Walden, pulling a mass of heterogeneous-looking papers out of his pocket. "Where can it be? Not that it matters; he will have supper and beds ready for us to-morrow night. And then," he went on to me, "if you like it you can make some arrangement for the time you wish to stay, if not you can return here, or go on to any place that takes your fancy. We, my wife and I and these boys, must be home by Saturday afternoon, so we can only stay the one night at Silberbach," for this was Thursday.

And so it was settled.

The next day dawned as bright and cloudless as its predecessors. The gentlemen had started—I should be afraid to say how early—meaning to be overtaken by us at Ulrichsthal. Reggie had gone to bed with the firm intention of accompanying them, but as it was not easy to wake him and get him up in time to eat his breakfast, and be ready when the Einspänner came round to the door, my predictions that he would be too sleepy for so early a start proved true.

It was pleasant in the early morning—pleasanter than it would be later in the day. I noticed an unusual amount of blue haze on the distant mountain-tops, for the road along which we were driving was open on all sides for some distance, and the view was extensive.

"That betokens great heat, I suppose," I said, pointing out the appearance I observed to my companion.

"I suppose so. That bluish mist probably increases in hot and sultry weather," she said. "But it is always to be seen more or less in this country, and is, I believe, peculiar to some of the German hill and forest districts. I don't know what it comes from—whether it has to do with the immense number of pines in the forests, perhaps. Some one, I think, once told me that it indicates the presence of a great deal of electricity in the air, but I am far too ignorant to know if that is true or not."

"And I am far too ignorant to know what the effect would be if it were so," I said. "It is a very healthy country, is it not?"

"For strangers it certainly is. Doctors send their patients here from all parts of Germany. But the inhabitants themselves do not seem strong or healthy. One sees a good many deformed people, and they all look pale and thin—much less robust than the people of the Black Forest. But that may come from their poverty—the peasants of the Black Forest are proverbially well off."

A distant, very distant, peal of thunder was heard at this moment.

"I hope the weather is not going to break up just yet," I said. "Are there often bad thunderstorms here?"

"Yes; I think we do have a good many in this part of the world," she replied. "But I do not think there are any signs of one at present."

And then, still a little sleepy and tired from our unusual exertions of the last three days, we all three, Frau von Walden, Nora, and myself, sat very still for some time, though the sound of Reggie's voice persistently endeavouring to make the driver understand his inquiries, showed that he was as lively as ever.

He turned round after a while in triumph.

"Mamma, Frau von Walden," he exclaimed, "we are close to that place where they make the cups and saucers. Herr von Walden said we weren't to forget to go there—and you all would have forgotten, you see, if it hadn't been for me," he added complacently.

"Grünstein," said Frau von Walden. "Well, tell the driver to stop there, he can rest his horses for half an hour or so; and thank you for reminding us, Reggie, for I should have been sorry to lose the opportunity of matching my service."

The china manufactory was not of any very remarkable interest, at least not for those who had visited such places before. But the people were exceedingly civil, and evidently very pleased to have visitors; and while my friend was looking out the things she was specially in search of—a business which promised to take some little time—a good-natured sub-manager, or functionary of some kind, proposed to take the children to see the sheds where the first mixing and kneading took place, the moulding rooms, the painting rooms, the ovens—in short, the whole process. They accepted his offer with delight, and I wandered about the various pattern or show rooms, examining and admiring all that was to be seen, poking into corners where any specially pretty bit of china caught my eye. But there was no great variety in design or colour, though both were good of their kind, the Grünsteiners, like their rivals of Blauenstein, seeming content to follow in the steps of their fathers without seeking for new inspirations. Suddenly, however, all but hidden in a corner, far away back on a shelf, a flash of richer tints made me start forward eagerly. There was no one near to apply to at the moment, so I carefully drew out my treasure trove. It was a cup and saucer, evidently of the finest quality of china, though pretty similar in shape to the regular Grünstein ware, but in colouring infinitely richer—really beautiful, with an almost Oriental cleverness in the blending of the many shades, and yet decidedly more striking and uncommon than any of the modern Oriental with which of late years the facilities of trade with the East make us so familiar. I stood with the cup in my hand, turning it around and admiring it, when Frau von Walden and the woman who had been attending to her orders came forward to where I was.

"See here," I exclaimed; "here is a lovely cup! Now a service like that would be tempting! Have you more of it?" I inquired of the woman.

She shook her head.

"That is all that remains," she said. "We have never kept it in stock; it is far too expensive. Of course it can be made to order, though it would take some months, and cost a good deal."

"I wish I could order a service of it," I said; but when I heard how much it would probably cost it was my turn to shake my head. "No, I must consider about it," I decided; "but I really have never seen anything prettier. Can I buy this cup?"

The woman hesitated.

"It is the only one left," she said; "but I think—oh yes, I feel sure—we have the pattern among the painting designs. This cup belonged to, or rather was an extra one of, a tea-service made expressly for the Duchess of T—, on her marriage, now some years ago. And it is curious, we sold the other one— there were two too many—to a compatriot of yours (the gracious lady is English?) two or three years ago. He admired them so much, and felt sure his mother would send an order if he took it home to show her. A tall, handsome young man he was. I remember it so well; just about this time of the year, and hot, sultry weather like this. He was travelling on foot—for pleasure, no doubt—for he had quite the air of a milord. And he bought the cup, and took it with him. But he has never written! I made sure he would have done so."

"He did not leave his name or address?" I said; for the world is a small place: it was just possible I might have known him, and the little coincidence would have been curious.

"Oh no," said the woman. "But I have often wondered why he changed his mind. He seemed so sure about sending the order. It was not the price that made him hesitate; but he wished his lady mother to make out the list herself."

"Well, I confess the price does make me hesitate," I said, smiling. "However, if you will let me buy this cup, I have great hopes of proving a better customer than my faithless compatriot."

"I am sure he meant to send the order," said the woman. She spoke quite civilly, but I was not sure that she liked my calling him "faithless."

"It is evident," I said to Frau von Walden, "that the good-looking young Englishman made a great impression on her. I rather think she gave him the fellow cup for nothing."

But after all I had no reason to be jealous, for just then the woman returned, after consulting the manager, to tell me I might have the cup and saucer, and for a less sum than their real worth, seeing that I was taking it, in a sense, as a pattern.

Then she wrapped it up for me, carefully and in several papers, of which the outside one was bright blue; and, very proud of my acquisition, I followed Frau von Walden to the other side of the building containing the workrooms, where we found the two children full of interest about all they had seen.

I should here, perhaps, apologise for entering into so much and apparently trifling detail. But as will, I think, be seen when I have told all I have to tell, it would be difficult to give the main facts fairly, and so as to avoid all danger of any mistaken impression, without relating the whole of the surroundings. If I tried to condense, to pick out the salient points, to enter into no particulars but such as directly and unmistakably lead up to the central interest, I might unintentionally omit what those wiser than I would consider as bearing on it. So, like a patient adjured by his doctor, or a client urged by his lawyer, to tell the whole at the risk of long-windedness, I prefer to run that risk, while claiming my readers' forgiveness for so doing, rather than that of relating my story incompletely.

And what I would here beg to have specially observed is that not one word about the young Englishman had been heard by Nora. She was, in fact, in a distant part of the building at the time the saleswoman was telling us about him. And, furthermore, I am equally certain, and so is Frau von Walden, that neither she nor I, then or afterwards, mentioned the subject to, or in the presence of, the children. I did not show her the cup and saucer, as it would have been a pity to undo its careful wrappings. All she knew about it will be told in due course.

We had delayed longer than we intended at the china manufactory, and in consequence we were somewhat late at the meeting-place—Ulrichsthal. The gentlemen had arrived there quite an hour before; so they had ordered luncheon, or dinner rather, at the inn, and thoroughly explored the ruins. But dinner discussed, and neither Frau von Walden nor I objecting to pipes, our cavaliers were amiably willing to show us all there was to be seen.

The ruins were those of an ancient monastery, one of the most ancient in Germany, I believe. They covered a very large piece of ground, and had they been in somewhat better preservation, they would have greatly impressed us; as it was they were undoubtedly, even to the unlearned in archæological lore, very interesting. The position of the monastery had been well and carefully chosen, for on one side it commanded a view of surpassing beauty over the valley through which we had travelled from Seeberg, while on the other arose still higher ground, richly wooded, for the irrepressible forest here, as it were, broke out again.

"It is a most lovely spot!" I said with some enthusiasm, as we sat in the shade of the ruined cloisters, the sunshine flecking the sward in eccentric patches as it made its way through what had evidently been richly-sculptured windows. "How one wishes it were possible to see it as it must have been—how many?—three or four hundred years ago, I suppose!"

Lutz grunted.

"What did you say, Lutz?" asked his mother.

"Nothing particular," he sighed. "I was only thinking of what I read in the guide-book, that the monastery was destroyed—partly by lightning, I believe, all the same—by order of the authorities, in consequence of the really awful wickedness of the monks who inhabited it. So I am not sure that it would have been a very nice place to visit at the time you speak of, gracious lady, begging your pardon."

"What a pity!" I said, with a little shudder. "I do not like to think of it. And I was going to say how beautiful it must be here in the moonlight! But now that you have disenchanted me, Lutz, I should not like it at all," and I arose as I spoke.

"Why not, mamma?" said Reggie curiously. I had not noticed that he and his sister were listening to us. "They're not here now—not those naughty monks."

"No, of course not," agreed practical Nora. "Mamma only means that it is a pity such a beautiful big house as this must have been had to be pulled down—such a waste when there are so many poor people in the world with miserable, little, stuffy houses, or none at all even! That was what you meant; wasn't it, mamma?"

"It is always a pity—the worst of pities—when people are wicked, wherever they are," I replied.

"But all monks are not bad," remarked Nora consolingly. "Think of the Great St. Bernard ones, with their dogs."

And on Reggie's inquiring mind demanding further particulars on the subject, she walked on with him somewhat in front of the rest of us, a happy little pair in the sunshine.

"Lutz," said his father, "you cannot be too careful what you say before children; they are often shocked or frightened by so little. Though yours are such healthy-minded little people," he added, turning to me, "it is not likely anything undesirable would make any impression on them."

I particularly remember this little incident.

It turned out a long walk to Silberbach, the longest we had yet attempted. Hitherto Herr von Walden had been on known ground, and thoroughly acquainted with the roads, the distances, and all necessary particulars; but it was the first time he had explored beyond Seeberg, and before we had accomplished more than half the journey, he began to feel a little alarm at the information given us by the travellers we came across at long intervals "coming from," not "going to St. Ives!" For the farther we went the greater seemed to be the distance we had to go!

"An hour or thereabouts," grew into "two," or even "three" hours; and at last, on a peculiarly stupid countryman assuring us we would scarcely reach our destination before nightfall, our conductor's patience broke down altogether.

"Idiots!" he exclaimed. "But I cannot stand this any longer. I will hasten on and see for myself; and if, as I expect, we are really not very far from Silberbach, it will be all the better for me to find out the 'Katze,' and see that everything is ready for your arrival."

Frau von Walden seemed a little inclined to protest, but I begged her not to do so, seeing that three able-bodied protectors still remained to us, and that it probably was really tiresome for a remarkably good and trained pedestrian like her husband to have to adapt his vigorous steps to ours. And comfort came from an unexpected quarter. The old peasant woman, strong and muscular as any English labourer, whom we had hired at Seeberg to carry our bags and shawls through the forest, overheard the discussion, and for the first time broke silence to assure "the gracious ladies" that Silberbach was at no great distance; in half an hour or so we should come upon the first of its houses.

"Though as for the 'Katze,'" she added, "that was farther off—at the other end of the village;" and she went on muttering something about "if she had known we were going to the 'Katze,'" which we did not understand, but which afterwards, "being translated," proved to mean that she would have stood out for more pay.

Sure enough, at the end of not more than three-quarters of an hour we came upon one or two outlying houses. Then the trees gradually here grew sparser, and soon ceased, except in occasional patches. It was growing dusk; but as we emerged from the wood we found that we were on a height, the forest road having been a steady, though almost imperceptible, ascent. Far below gleamed already some twinkling cottage lights, and the silvery reflection of a small piece of water.

"To be sure," said young von Trachenfels, "there is a lake at Silberbach. Here we are at last! But where is the 'Katze'?"

He might well ask. Never was there so tantalising a place as Silberbach. Instead of one compact, sensible village, it was more like three or four—nay, five or six—wretched hamlets, each at several minutes' distance from all the others. And the "Katze," of course, was at the farther end of the farthest off from where we stood of these miserable little ragged ends of village! Climbing is tiring work, but it seemed to me it would have been preferable to what lay before us,—a continual descent, by the ruggedest of hill-paths, of nearly two miles, stumbling along in the half light, tired, footsore past description, yet—to our everlasting credit be it recorded—laughing, or trying to laugh, determined at all costs to make the best of it.

"I have no feet left," said poor Frau von Walden. "I am only conscious of two red-hot balls attached somehow to my ankles. I daresay they will drop off soon."

How thankful we were at last to attain to what bore some faint resemblance to a village street! How we gazed on every side to discover anything like an inn! How we stared at each other in bewilderment when at last, from we could not see where, came the well-known voice of Herr von Walden, shouting to us to stop.

"It is here—here, I say. You are going too far."

"Here," judging by the direction whence came the words, seemed to be a piled-up mass of hay, of proportions, exaggerated perhaps by the uncertain light, truly enormous. Was our friend buried in the middle of it? Not so. By degrees we made out his sunburnt face, beaming as ever, from out of a window behind the hay—cartful or stack, we were not sure which; and by still further degrees we discovered that the hay was being unloaded before a little house which it had almost entirely hidden from view, and inside which it was being carried, apparently by the front door, for there was no other door to be seen; but as we stood in perplexity, Herr von Walden, whose face had disappeared, emerged in some mysterious way.

"You can come through the kitchen, ladies; or by the window, if you please." But though the boys and Nora were got, or got themselves, in through the window, Frau von Walden and I preferred the kitchen; and I remember nothing more till we found ourselves all assembled—the original eight as we had started—in a very low-roofed, sandy-floored, tobacco-impregnated sort of cabin which, it appeared, was the salle-à-manger of the renowned hostelry "zur Katze" of Silberbach!

Herr von Walden was vigorously mopping his face. It was very red, and naturally so, considering the weather and the want of ventilation peculiar to the "Katze"; but it struck me there was something slightly forced about the beaminess.

"So, so," he began; "all's well that ends well! But I must explain," and he mopped still more vigorously, "that—there has been a slight, in short, a little, mistake about the accommodation I wish to secure. The supper I have seen to, and it will be served directly. But as to the beds," and here he could not help laughing, "our worthy host has beds enough"—we found afterwards that every available mattress and pillow in the village had been levied—"but there is but one bedroom, or two, I may say." For the poor Herr had not lost his time since his arrival. Appalled by the want of resources, he had suggested the levy of beds, and had got the host to spread them on the floor of a granary for himself, the three young men, and Reggie; while his wife, Nora, and I were to occupy the one bedroom, which luckily contained two small beds and a sort of settee, such as one sees in old farmhouses all over the world.

So it was decided; and, after all, for one night, what did it matter? For one night? that was for me the question! The supper was really not bad; but the look, and still worse the smell, of the room where it was served, joined no doubt to our excessive fatigue, made it impossible for me to eat anything. My friends were sorry, and I felt ashamed of myself for being so easily knocked up or knocked down. How thoroughly I entered into Frau von Walden's honestly-expressed dislike to "roughing it"! Yet it was not only the uncivilised look of the place, nor the coarse food, nor the want of comfort that made me feel that one night of Silberbach would indeed be enough for me. A sort of depression, of fear almost, came over me when I pictured the two children and myself alone in that strange, out-of-the-world place, where it really seemed to me we might all three be made an end of without any one being the wiser of it! There was a general look of squalor and stolid depression about the people too: the landlord was a black-browed, surlily silent sort of man, his wife and the one maid-servant looked frightened and anxious, and the only voices to be heard were those of half-tipsy peasants drinking and quarrelling at the bar.

To say the least, it was not enlivening. Yet my pride was aroused. I did not like to own myself already beaten. After supper I sat apart, reflecting rather gloomily as to what I could or should do, while the young men and the children amused themselves with the one piece of luxury with which the poorest inn in Thuringia is sure to be provided. For, anomalous as it may seem, there was a piano, and by no means an altogether decrepit one, in the sandy-floored parlour!

Herr von Walden was smoking his pipe outside, the hay being by this time housed somewhere or other. His wife, who had been speaking to him, came in and sat down beside me.

"My dear," she said, "you must not be vexed with me for renewing the subject, but I cannot help it; I feel a responsibility. You must not, you really must not, think of staying here alone with those two children. It is not fit for you."

Oh, how I blessed her for breaking the ice! I could hardly help hugging her as I replied—diplomatically—

"You really think so?"

"Certainly I do; and so, though perhaps he won't say so as frankly—so does my husband. He says I am foolish and fanciful; but I confess to feeling a kind of dislike to the place that I cannot explain. Perhaps there is thunder in the air—that always affects my nerves—but I just feel that I cannot agree to your staying on here."

"Very well, I am quite willing to go back to Seeberg to-morrow," I replied meekly. "Of course we can't judge of the place by what we have seen of it to-night, but no doubt, as far as the inn is concerned, Seeberg is much nicer. I daresay we can see all we want by noon to-morrow, and get back to Seeberg in the afternoon."

Kind Frau von Walden kissed me rapturously on both cheeks.

"You don't know, my dear, the relief to my mind of hearing you say so! And now I think the best thing we can do is to go to bed. For we must start at six."

"So early!" I exclaimed, with a fresh feeling of dismay.

"Yes, indeed; and I must bid you good-bye to-night, for after all I am not to sleep in your room, which is much better, as I should have had to disturb you so early. My husband has found a tidy room next door in a cottage, and we shall do very well there."

What sort of a place she euphemistically described as "a tidy room" I never discovered. But it would have been useless to remonstrate, the kind creature was so afraid of incommoding us that she would have listened to no objections.

Herr von Walden came in just as we were about to wish each other good-night.

"So!" he said, with a tone of amiable indulgence, "so! And what do you think of Silberbach? My wife feels sure you will not like it after all."

"I think I shall see as much as I care to see of it in an hour or two to-morrow morning," I replied quietly. "And by the afternoon the children and I will go back to our comfortable quarters at Seeberg."

"Ah, indeed! Yes, I daresay it will be as well," he said airily, as if he had nothing at all to do with decoying us to the place. "Then good-night and pleasant dreams, and—"

"But," I interrupted, "I want to know how we are to get back to Seeberg. Can I get an Einspänner here?"

"To be sure, to be sure. You have only to speak to the landlord in the morning, and tell him at what hour you want it," he answered so confidently that I felt no sort of misgiving, and I turned with a smile to finish my good-nights.

The young men were standing close beside us. I shook hands with Trachenfels and Lutz, the latter of whom, though he replied as heartily as usual, looked, I thought, annoyed. George Norman followed me to the door of the room. In front of us was the ladder-like staircase leading to the upper regions.

"What a hole of a place!" said the boy. "I don't mind quite a cottage if it's clean and cheerful, but this place is so grim and squalid. I can't tell you how glad I am you're not going to stay on here alone. It really isn't fit for you."

"Well, you may be easy, as we shall only be here a few hours after you leave."

"Yes; so much the better. I wish I could have stayed, but I must be back at Kronberg to-morrow. Lutz could have stayed and seen you back to Seeberg, but his father won't let him. Herr von Walden is so queer once he takes an idea in his head—and he won't allow this place isn't all right."

"But I daresay there would be nothing to hurt us! Anyway, I will write to reassure you that we have not fallen into a nest of cut-throats or brigands," I said laughingly.

Certainly it never occurred to me or to my friends what would be the nature of the "experience" which would stamp Silberbach indelibly on our memory.

We must have been really very tired, for, quite contrary to our habit, the children and I slept late the next morning, undisturbed by the departure of our friends at the early hour arranged by them.

The sun was shining, and Silberbach, like every other place, appeared all the better for it. But the view from the window of our room was not encouraging. It looked out upon the village street—a rough, unkempt sort of track—and on its other side the ground rose abruptly to some height, but treeless and grassless. It seemed more like the remains of a quarry of some kind, for there was nothing to be seen but stones and broken pieces of rock.

"We must go out after our breakfast and look about us a little before we start," I said. "But how glad I shall be to get back to that bright, cheerful Seeberg!"

"Yes, indeed," said Nora. "I think this is the ugliest place I ever was at in my life." And she was not inclined to like it any better when Reggie, whom we sent down to reconnoitre, came back to report that we must have our breakfast in our own room.

"There are a lot of rough-looking men down there, smoking and drinking beer. You couldn't eat there," said the child.

But, after all, it was to be our last meal there, and we did not complain. The root coffee was not too unpalatable with plenty of good milk; the bread was sour and the butter dubious, as Ottilia had foretold, so we soaked the bread in the coffee, like French peasants.

"Mamma," said Nora gravely, "it makes me sorry for poor people. I daresay many never have anything nicer to eat than this."

"Not nicer than this!" I exclaimed. "Why, my dear child, thousands, not in Germany only, but in France and England, never taste anything as good."

The little girl opened her eyes. There are salutary lessons to be learnt from even the mildest experience of "roughing it."

Suddenly Nora's eyes fell on a little parcel in blue paper. It was lying on one of the shelves of the stove, which, as in most German rooms, stood out a little from the wall, and in its summer idleness was a convenient receptacle for odds and ends. This stove was a high one, of black-leaded iron; it stood between the door and the wall, on the same side as the door, and was the most conspicuous object in the room.

"Mamma," she exclaimed, "there is the parcel you brought away from the china place. What is it? I wish you would show it me."

I gave a little exclamation of annoyance.

"Frau von Walden has forgotten it," I said; for my friend, returning straight to Kronberg, had offered to take it home for me in her bag for fear of accidents. "It does not matter," I added, "I will pack it among our soft things. It is a very pretty cup and saucer, but I will show it to you at Kronberg, for it is so nicely wrapped up. Now I am going downstairs to order the Einspänner, and we can walk about for an hour or two."

The children came with me. I had some trouble in disinterring the landlord, but at last I found him, of course with a pipe in his mouth, hanging about the premises. He listened to me civilly enough, but when I waited for his reply as to whether the Einspänner would be ready about twelve o'clock, he calmly regarded me without speaking. I repeated my inquiry.

"At twelve?" he said calmly. "Yes, no doubt the gracious lady might as well fix twelve as any other hour, for there was no such thing as a horse, much less an Einspänner, to be had at Silberbach."

I stared at him in my turn.

"No horse, no carriage to be had! How do people ever get away from here then?" I said.

"They don't get away—that is to say, if they come at all, they go as they came, in the carriage that brought them; otherwise they neither come nor go. The lady came on foot: she can go on foot; otherwise she can stay."

There seemed something sinister in his words. A horrible, ridiculous feeling came over me that we were caught in a net, as it were, and doomed to stay at Silberbach for the rest of our lives. But I looked at the man. He was simply stolid and indifferent. I did not believe then, nor do I now, that he was anything worse than sulky and uncivilised. He did not even care to have us as his visitors: he had no wish to retain us nor to speed us on our way. Had we remained at the "Katze" from that day to this, I don't believe he would have ever inquired what we stayed for!

"I cannot walk back to Seeberg," I said half indignantly, "we are too tired; nor would it be safe through the forest alone with two children."

The landlord knocked some ashes off his pipe.

"There may be an ox-cart going that way next week," he observed.

"Next week!" I repeated. Then a sudden idea struck me. "Is there a post-office here?" I said.

Of course there was a post-office; where can one go in Germany where there is not a post and telegraph office?

"The telegraph officials must be sadly overworked here," I said to myself. But as far as mine host was concerned, I satisfied myself with obtaining the locality of the post-office, and with something like a ray of hope I turned to look for the children. They had been amusing themselves with the piano in the now empty room, but as I called to them, Reggie ran out with a very red face.

"I wish I were a man, mamma. Fancy! a peasant—one of those men who were drinking beer—came and put his arm around Nora as she was playing. 'Du spielst schön,' he said, and I do believe he meant to kiss her, if I hadn't shaken my fist at him."

"Yes, indeed, mamma," said Nora, equally but more calmly indignant. "I certainly think the sooner we get away the better."

I had to tell them of my discomfiture, but ended with my new idea.

"If there is a post-office," I said, "the mail must stop there, and the mail takes passengers."

But, arrived at the neat little post-house—to reach which without a most tremendous round we had to climb up a really precipitous path, so called, over the stones and rocks in front of the inn—new dismay awaited us. The postmaster was a very old man, but of a very different type from our host. He was sorry to disappoint us, but the mail only stopped here for letters—all passengers must begin their journey at—I forget where—leagues off on the other side from Silberbach. We wanted to get away? He was not surprised. What had we come for? No one ever came here. Were we Americans! Staying at the "Katze"! Good heavens! "A rough place." "I should rather think so."

And this last piece of information fairly overcame him. He evidently felt he must come to the rescue of these poor Babes in the wood.

"Come up when the mail passes from Seeberg this evening at seven, and I will see what I can do with the conductor. If he happens to have no passengers to-morrow, he may stretch a point and take you in. No one will be the wiser."

"Oh, thanks, thanks," I cried. "Of course I will pay anything he likes to ask."

"No need for that. He is a braver Mann, and will not cheat you."

"We shall be here at seven, then. I would rather have started to walk than stayed here indefinitely."

"Not to-day anyway. We shall have a storm," he said, looking up to the sky. "Adieu. Auf Wiedersehen!"

"I wish we had not to stay another night here," I said. "Still, to-morrow morning will soon come."

We spent the day as best we could. There was literally nothing to see, nowhere to go, except back into the forest whence we had come. Nor dared we go far, for the day grew more and more sultry; the strange, ominous silence that precedes a storm came on, adding to our feelings of restlessness and depression. And by about two o'clock, having ventured out again after "dinner," we were driven in by the first great drops. Huddled together in our cheerless little room we watched the breaking loose of the storm demons. I am not affected by thunder and lightning, nor do I dread them. But what a storm that was! Thunder, lightning, howling wind, and rain like no rain I had ever seen before, all mingled together. An hour after it began, a cart, standing high and dry in the steep village street, was hidden by water to above the top of the wheels—a little more and it would have floated like a boat. But by about five, things calmed down; the few stupid-looking peasants came out of their houses, and gazed about them as if to see what damage had been done. Perhaps it was not much after all—they seemed to take it quietly enough; and by six all special signs of disturbance had disappeared—the torrents melted away as if by magic. Only a strange, heavy mist began to rise, enveloping everything, so that we could hardly believe the evening was yet so early. I looked at my watch.

"Half-past six. We must, mist or no mist, go up to the post-house. But I don't mind going alone, dears."

"No, no, mamma; I must go with you, to take care of you," said Reggie; "but Nora needn't."

"Perhaps it would be as well," said the little girl. "I have one or two buttons to sew on, and I am still rather tired."

And, knowing she was never timid about being left alone, thinking we should be absent half an hour at most, I agreed.

But the half hour lengthened into an hour, then into an hour and a half, before the weary mail made its appearance. The road through the forest must be all but impassable, our old friend told us. But oh, how tired Reggie and I were of waiting! though all the time never a thought of uneasiness with regard to Nora crossed my mind. And when the mail did come, delayed, as the postmaster had suspected, the good result of his negotiations made us forget all our troubles; for the conductor all but promised to take us the next morning, in consideration of a very reasonable extra payment. It was most unlikely he would have any, certainly not many passengers. We must be there, at the post-house, by nine o'clock, baggage and all, for he dared not wait a moment, and he would do his best.

Through the evening dusk, now fast replacing the scattered mist, Reggie and I, light of heart, stumbled down the rocky path.

"How pleased Nora will be! She will be wondering what has come over us," I said as the "Katze" came in view. "But what is that, Reggie, running up and down in front of the house? Is it a sheep, or a big white dog? or—or a child? Can it be Nora, and no cloak or hat? and so damp and chilly as it is? How can she be so foolish?"

And with a vague uneasiness I hurried on.

Yes, it was Nora. There was light enough to see her face. What had happened to my little girl? She was white—no, not white, ghastly. Her eyes looked glassy, and yet as if drawn into her head; her whole bright, fearless bearing was gone. She clutched me convulsively as if she would never again let me go. Her voice was so hoarse that I could scarcely distinguish what she said.

"Send Reggie in—he must not hear," were her first words—of rare unselfishness and presence of mind.

"Reggie," I said, "tell the maid to take candles up to our room, and take off your wet boots at once."

My children are obedient; he was off instantly.

Then Nora went on, still in a strained, painful whisper—

"Mamma, there has been a man in our room, and—"

"Did that peasant frighten you again, dear? Oh, I am so sorry I left you;" for my mind at once reverted to the man whom Reggie had shaken his fist at that morning.

"No, no; not that. I would not have minded. But, mamma, Reggie must never know it—he is so little, he could not bear it—mamma, it was not a man. It was—oh, mamma, I have seen a ghost!"

PART II

"A ghost," I repeated, holding the poor trembling little thing more closely. I think my first sensation was a sort of rage at whomever or whatever—ghost or living being—had frightened her so terribly. "Oh, Nora darling, it couldn't be a ghost. Tell me about it, and I will try to find out what it was. Or would you rather try to forget about it just now, and tell me afterwards? You are shivering so dreadfully. I must get you warm first of all."

"But let me tell you, mamma—I must tell you," she entreated piteously. "If you could explain it, I should be so glad, but I am afraid you can't," and again a shudder passed through her.

I saw it was better to let her tell it. I had by this time drawn her inside; a door in front stood open, and a bright fire caught my eyes. It was the kitchen, and the most inviting-looking room in the house. I peeped in—there was no one there, but from an inner room we heard the voice of the landlady hushing her baby to sleep.

"Come to the fire, Nora," I said. Just then Reggie came clattering downstairs, followed by Lieschen, the taciturn "maid of the inn."

"She has taken a candle upstairs, mamma, but I've not taken off my boots, for there's a little calf, she says, in the stable, and she's going to show it me. May I go?"

"Yes, but don't stay long," I said, my opinion of the sombre Lieschen improving considerably; and when they were out of hearing, "Now, Nora dear, tell me what frightened you so."

"Mamma," she said, a little less white and shivering by now, but still with the strange strained look in her eyes that I could not bear to see, "it couldn't have been a real man. Listen, mamma. When you and Reggie went, I got out a needle and thread—out of your little bag—and first I mended a hole in my glove, and then I took off one of my boots—the buttoning-up-the-side ones, you know—to sew a button on. I soon finished it, and then, without putting my boot on, I sat there, looking out of the window and wondering if you and Reggie would soon be back. Then I thought perhaps I could see if you were coming, better from the window of the place outside our room, where the hay and bags of flour are." (I think I forgot to say that to get to our room we had to cross at the top of the stair a sort of landing, along one side of which, as Nora said, great bags of flour or grain and trusses of hay were ranged; this place had a window with a somewhat more extended view than that of our room.) "I went there, still without my boot, and I knelt in front of the window some time, looking up the rough path, and wishing you would come. But I was not the least dull or lonely. I was only a little tired. At last I got tired of watching there, and I thought I would come back to our room and look for something to do. The door was not closed, but I think I had half drawn it to as I came out. I pushed it open and went in, and then—I seemed to feel there was something that had not been there before, and I looked up; and just beside the stove—the door opens against the stove, you know, and so it had hidden it for a moment as it were—there, mamma, stood a man! I saw him as plainly as I see you. He was staring at the stove, afterwards I saw it must have been at your little blue paper parcel. He was a gentleman, mamma—quite young. I saw his coat, it was cut like George Norman's. I think he must have been an Englishman. His coat was dark, and bound with a little very narrow ribbon binding. I have seen coats like that. He had a dark blue neck-tie, his dress all looked neat and careful—like what all gentlemen are; I saw all that, mamma, before I clearly saw his face. He was tall and had fair hair—I saw that at once. But I was not frightened; just at first I did not even wonder how he could have got into the room—now I see he couldn't without my knowing. My first thought, it seems so silly," and Nora here smiled a little, "my first thought was, 'Oh, he will see I have no boot on,'"—which was very characteristic of the child, for Nora was a very "proper" little girl,—"and just as I thought that, he seemed to know I was there, for he slowly turned his head from the stove and looked at me, and then I saw his face. Oh, mamma!"

"Was there anything frightening about it?" I said.

"I don't know," the child went on. "It was not like any face I ever saw, and yet it does not sound strange. He had nice, rather wavy fair hair, and I think he must have been nice-looking. His eyes were blue, and he had a little fair moustache. But he was so fearfully pale, and a look over all that I can't describe. And his eyes when he looked at me seemed not to see me, and yet they turned on me. They looked dreadfully sad, and though they were so close to me, as if they were miles and miles away. Then his lips parted slightly, very slightly, as if he were going to speak. Mamma," Nora went on impressively, "they would have spoken if I had said the least word—I felt they would. But just then—and remember, mamma, it couldn't have been yet two seconds since I came in, I hadn't yet had time to get frightened— just then there came over me the most awful feeling. I knew it was not a real man, and I seemed to hear myself saying inside my mind, 'It is a ghost,' and while I seemed to be saying it—I had not moved my eyes—while I looked at him—"

"He disappeared?"

"No, mamma, he did not even disappear. He was just no longer there. I was staring at nothing! Then came a sort of wild fear. I turned and rushed downstairs, even without my boot, and all the way the horrible feeling was that even though he was no longer there he might still be coming after me. I should not have cared if there had been twenty tipsy peasants downstairs! But I found Lieschen. Of course I said nothing to her; I only asked her to come up with a light to help me to find my boot, and as soon as I had put it on I came outside, and ran up and down—it was a long time, I think—till you and Reggie came at last. Mamma, can you explain it?"

How I longed to be able to do so! But I would not deceive the child. Besides, it would have been useless.

"No, dear. As yet I cannot. But I will try to understand it. There are several ways it may be explained. Have you ever heard of optical delusions, Nora?"

"I am not sure. You must tell me;" and she looked at me so appealingly, and with such readiness to believe whatever I told her, that I felt I would give anything to restore her to her former happy fearlessness.

But just then Reggie came in from the stable.

"We must go upstairs," I said; "and Lieschen," turning to her, "bring up our supper at once. We are leaving very early to-morrow morning, and we will go early to bed."

"Oh, mamma," whispered Nora, "if only we had not to stay all night in that room!"

But there was no help for it, and she was thankful to hear of the success of our expedition to the post-office. During supper we, of course, on Reggie's account, said nothing of Nora's fright, but as soon as it was over, Reggie declaring himself very sleepy, we got him undressed and put to bed on the settee originally intended for Nora. He was asleep in five minutes, and then Nora and I did our utmost to arrive at the explanation we so longed for. We thoroughly examined the room; there was no other entrance, no cupboard of any kind even. I tried to imagine that some of our travelling cloaks or shawls hanging on the back of a chair might, in the uncertain light, have taken imaginary proportions; that the stove itself might have cast a shadow we had not before observed; I suggested everything, but in vain. Nothing shook Nora's conviction that she had seen something not to be explained.

"For the light was not uncertain just then," she maintained; "the mist had gone and it had not begun to get dark. And then I saw him so plainly! If it had been a fancy ghost it wouldn't have looked like that—it would have had a long white thing floating over it, and a face like a skeleton perhaps. But to see somebody just like a regular gentleman—I could never have fancied that!"

There was a good deal in what she said. I had to give up my suggestions, and I tried to give Nora some idea of what are called "optical delusions," though my own comprehension of the theory was of the vaguest. She listened, but I don't think my words had much weight. And at last I told her I thought she had better go to bed and try to sleep. I saw she shrank from the idea, but it had to be.

"We can't sit up all night, I suppose," she said, "but I wish we could. I am so dreadfully afraid of waking in the night, and—and—seeing him there again."

"Would you like to sleep in my bed? though it is so tiny, I could make room and put you inside," I said.

Nora looked wistfully at the haven of refuge, but her good sense and considerateness for me came to the front.

"No," she said, "neither of us would sleep, and you would be so tired to-morrow. I will get into my own bed, and I will try to sleep, mamma."

"And listen, Nora; if you are the least frightened in the night, or if you can't sleep, call out to me without hesitation. I am sure to wake often, and I will speak to you from time to time."

That was the longest night of my life! The first part was not the worst. By what I really thought a fortunate chance it was a club night of some kind at Silberbach—a musical club, of course; and all the musically-gifted peasants of the countryside assembled in the sanded parlour of the "Katze." The noise was something indescribable, for though there may have been some good voices among them, they were drowned in the din. But though it prevented us from sleeping, it also fairly drove away all ghostly alarms. By twelve o'clock or thereabouts the party seemed to disperse, and all grew still. Then came some hours I can never forget. There was faint moonlight by fits and starts, and I not only found it impossible to sleep, I found it impossible to keep my eyes shut. Some irresistible fascination seemed to force them open, and obliged me ever and anon to turn in the direction of the stove, from which, however, before going to bed, I had removed the blue paper parcel. And each time I did so I said to myself, "Am I going to see that figure standing there as Nora saw it? Shall I remain sane if I do? Shall I scream out? Will it look at me, in turn, with its sad unearthly eyes? Will it speak? If it moves across the room and comes near me, or if I see it going towards Nora, or leaning over my Reggie sleeping there in his innocence, misdoubting of no fateful presence near, what, oh! what shall I do?"

For in my heart of hearts, though I would not own it to Nora, I felt convinced that what she had seen was no living human being—whence it had come, or why, I could not tell. But in the quiet of the night I had thought of what the woman at the china factory had told us, of the young Englishman who had bought the other cup, who had promised to write and never done so! What had become of him? "If," I said to myself, "if I had the slightest reason to doubt his being at this moment alive and well in his own country, as he pretty certainly is, I should really begin to think he had been robbed and murdered by our surly landlord, and that his spirit had appeared to us—the first compatriots who have passed this way since, most likely—to tell the story."

I really think I must have been a little light-headed some part of that night. My poor Nora, I am certain, never slept, but I can only hope her imagination was less wildly at work than mine. From time to time I spoke to her, and every time she was awake, for she always answered without hesitation.

"I am quite comfortable, dear mamma, and I don't think I am very frightened;" or else, "I have not slept much, but I have said my prayers a great many times, and all the hymns I could remember. Don't mind about me, mamma, and do try to sleep."

I watched the dawn slowly breaking. From where I lay I could see through the window the high mound of rough stones and fragments of rock that I have described. At its foot there was a low wall loosely constructed of these same unhewn blocks, and the shapes that evolved themselves out of this wall, beside which grew two or three stunted trees, were more grotesque and extraordinary than I could describe. They varied like the colours in a kaleidoscope with the wavering and increasing light. At one time it seemed to me that one of the trees was a gipsy woman enveloped in a cloak, extending her arm towards me threateningly; at another, two weird dogs seemed to be fighting together; but however fantastic and fearsome had been these strange effects of light and fancy mingled together, I should not have minded—I knew what they were; it was a relief to have anything to look at which could keep my eyes from constantly turning in the direction of that black iron stove.

I fell asleep at last, though not for long. When I woke it was bright morning—fresher and brighter, I felt, as I threw open the window, than the day before. With the greatest thankfulness that the night was over at last, as soon as I was dressed I began to put our little belongings together, and then turned to awake the children. Nora was sleeping quietly; it seemed a pity to arouse her, for it was not much past six, but I heard the people stirring about downstairs, and I had a feverish desire to get away; for though the daylight had dispersed much of the "eerie" impression of Nora's fright, there was a feeling of uneasiness, almost of insecurity, left in my mind since recalling the incident of the young man who had visited the china factory. How did I know but that some harm had really come to him in this very place? There was certainly nothing about the landlord to inspire confidence. At best it was a strange and unpleasant coincidence. The evening before I had half thought of inquiring of the landlord or his wife, or even of Lieschen, if any English had ever before stayed at the "Katze." If assured by them that we were the first, or at least the first "in their time," it would, I thought, help to assure Nora that the ghost had really been a delusion of some kind. But then, again, supposing the people of the inn hesitated to reply—supposing the landlord to be really in any way guilty, and my inquiries were to rouse his suspicions, would I not be risking dangerous enmity, besides strengthening the painful impression left on my own mind, and this corroboration of her own fear might be instinctively suspected by Nora, even if I told her nothing?

"No," I decided; "better leave it a mystery, in any case, till we are safely away from here." For, allowing that these people are perfectly innocent and harmless, their even telling me simply, like the woman at Grünstein, that such a person had been here, that he had fallen ill, possibly died here—I would rather not know it. It is certainly not probable that it was so; they would have been pretty sure to gossip about any occurrence of the kind, taciturn though they are. The wife would have talked of it to me—she is more genial than the others—for I had had a little kindly chat with her the day before, à propos of what every mother, of her class at least, is ready to talk about—the baby! A pretty baby too, though the last, she informed me with a sort of melancholy pride, of four she had "buried"—using the same expression in her rough German as a Lancashire factory hand or an Irish peasant woman—one after the other. Certainly Silberbach was not a cheerful or cheering spot. "No, no," I made up my mind, "I would rather at present know nothing, even if there is anything to know. I can the more honestly endeavour to remove the impression left on Nora."

The little girl was so easily awakened that I was half inclined to doubt if she had not been "shamming" out of filial devotion. She looked ill still, but infinitely better than the night before, and she so eagerly agreed with me in my wish to leave the house as soon as possible, that I felt sure it was the best thing to do. Reggie woke up rosy and beaming—evidently no ghosts had troubled his night's repose. There was something consoling and satisfactory in seeing him quite as happy and hearty as in his own English nursery. But though he had no uncanny reasons like us for disliking Silberbach, he was quite as cordial in his readiness to leave it. We got hold of Lieschen, and asked for our breakfast at once. As I had told the landlady the night before that we were leaving very early, our bill came up with the coffee. It was, I must say, moderate in the extreme—ten or twelve marks, if I remember rightly, for two nights' lodging and almost two days' board for three people. And such as it was, they had given us of their best. I felt a little twinge of conscience, when I said good-bye to the poor woman, for having harboured any doubts of the establishment. But when the gruff landlord, standing outside the door, smoking of course, nodded a surly "adieu" in return to our parting greeting, my feeling of unutterable thankfulness that we were not to spend another night under his roof regained the ascendant.

"Perhaps he is offended at my not having told him how I mean to get away, notwithstanding his stupidity about it," I said to myself, as we passed him. But no, there was no look of vindictiveness, of malice, of even annoyance on his dark face. Nay, more, I could almost have fancied there was the shadow of a smile as Reggie tugged at his Tam o' Shanter by way of a final salute. That landlord was really one of the most incomprehensible human beings it has ever been my fate to come across, in fact or fiction.

We had retained Lieschen to carry our modest baggage to the post-house, and having deposited it at the side of the road just where the coach stopped, she took her leave, apparently more than satisfied with the small sum of money I gave her, and civilly wishing us a pleasant journey. But though less gruff, she was quite as impassive as the landlord. She never asked where we were going, if we were likely ever to return again, and like her master, as I said, had we been staying there still, I do not believe she would ever have made an inquiry or expressed the slightest astonishment.

"There is really something very queer about Silberbach," I could not help saying to Nora, "both about the place and the people. They almost give one the feeling that they are half-witted, and yet they evidently are not. This last day or two I seem to have been living in a sort of dream or nightmare, and I shall not get over it altogether till we are fairly out of the place;" and though she said little, I felt sure the child understood me.

We were of course far, far too early for the post. The old man came out of his house, and seemed amused at our haste to be gone.

"I am afraid Silberbach has not taken your fancy," he said. "Well, no wonder. I think it is the dreariest place I ever saw."

"Then you do not belong to it? Have you not been here long?" I asked.

He shook his head.

"Only a few months, and I hope to get removed soon," he said. So he could have told me nothing, evidently! "It is too lonely here. There is not a creature in the place who ever touches a book—they are all as dull and stupid as they can be. But then they are very poor, and they live on here from year's end to year's end, barely able to earn their daily bread. Poverty degrades—there is no doubt of it, whatever the wise men may say. A few generations of it makes men little better than—" He stopped.

"Than?" I asked.

"Than," the old philosopher of the post-house went on, "pardon the expression—than pigs."

There were two or three of the fraternity grubbing about at the side of the road; they may have suggested the comparison. I could hardly help smiling.

"But I have travelled a good deal in Germany," I said, "and I have never anywhere found the people so stupid and stolid and ungenial as here."

"Perhaps not," he said. "Still there are many places like this, only naturally they are not the places strangers visit. It is never so bad where there are a few country houses near, for nowadays it must be allowed it is seldom but that the gentry take some interest in the people."

"It is a pity no rich man takes a fancy to Silberbach," I said.

"That day will never come. The best thing would be for a railway to be cut through the place, but that, too, is not likely."

Then the old postmaster turned into his garden, inviting us civilly to wait there or in the office if we preferred. But we liked better to stay outside, for just above the post-house there was a rather tempting little wood, much prettier than anything to be seen on the other side of the village. And Nora and I sat there quietly on the stumps of some old trees, while Reggie found a pleasing distraction in alternately chasing and making friends with a party of ducks, which, for reasons best known to themselves, had deserted their native element and come for a stroll in the woods.

From where we sat we looked down on our late habitation; we could almost distinguish the landlord's slouching figure and poor Lieschen with a pail of water slung at each side as she came in from the well.

"What a life!" I could not help saying. "Day after day nothing but work. I suppose it is not to be wondered at if they grow dull and stolid, poor things." Then my thoughts reverted to what up here in the sunshine and the fresh morning air and with the pleasant excitement of going away I had a little forgotten—the strange experience of the evening before. It was difficult for me now to realise that I had been so affected by it. I felt now as if I wished I could see the poor ghost for myself, and learn if there was aught we could do to serve or satisfy him! For in the old orthodox ghost-stories there is always some reason for these eerie wanderers returning to the world they have left. But when I turned to Nora and saw her dear little face still white and drawn, and with an expression half-subdued, half-startled, that it had never worn before, I felt thankful that the unbidden visitor had attempted no communication.

"It might have sent her out of her mind," I thought. "Why, if he had anything to say, did he appear to her, poor child, and not to me?—though, after all, I am not at all sure that I should not have gone out of my mind in such a case."

Before long the post-horn made itself heard in the distance; we hurried down, our hearts beating with the fear of possible disappointment. It was all right, however, there were no passengers, and nodding adieu to our old friend, we joyfully mounted into our places, and were bowled away to Seeberg.

There and at other spots in its pretty neighbourhood we pleasantly enough spent two or three weeks. Nora by degrees recovered her roses and her good spirits. Still, her strange experience left its mark on her. She was never again quite the merry, thoughtless, utterly fearless child she had been. I tried, however, to take the good with the ill, remembering that thorough-going childhood cannot last for ever, that the shock possibly helped to soften and modify a nature that might have been too daring for perfect womanliness—still more, wanting perhaps in tenderness and sympathy for the weaknesses and tremors of feebler temperaments.

At Kronberg, on our return, we found that Herr von Walden was off on a tour to the Italian lakes, Lutz and young Trachenfels had returned to their studies at Heidelberg, George Norman had gone home to England. All the members of our little party were dispersed except Frau von Walden.

To her and to Ottilia I told the story, sitting together one afternoon over our coffee, when Nora was not with us. It impressed them both. Ottilia could not resist an "I told you so."

"I knew, I felt," she said, "that something disagreeable would happen to you there. I never will forget," she went on naïvely, "the dreary, dismal impression the place left on me the only time I was there—pouring rain and universal gloom and discomfort. We had to wait there a few hours to get one of the horses shod, once when I was driving with my father from Seeberg to Marsfeldt."

Frau von Walden and I could not help smiling at her. Still there was no smiling at my story, though both agreed that, viewed in the light of unexaggerated common sense, it was most improbable that there was any tragedy mixed up with the disappearance of the young man we had heard of at Grünstein.

"And indeed why we should speak of his 'disappearance' I don't know," said Frau von Walden. "He did not write to send the order he had spoken of—that was all. No doubt he is very happy at his own home. When you are back in England, my dear, you must try to find him out—perhaps by means of the cup. And then when Nora sees him, and finds he is not at all like the 'ghost,' it will make her the more ready to think it was really only some very strange, I must admit, kind of optical delusion."

"But Nora has never heard the Grünstein story, and is not to hear it," said Ottilia.

"And England is a wide place, small as it is in one sense," I said. "Still, if I did come across the young man, I half think I would tell Nora the whole, and by showing her how my imagination had dressed it up, I think I could perhaps lessen the effect on her of what she thought she saw. It would prove to her better than anything, the tricks that fancy may play us.

"And in the meantime, if you take my advice, you will allude to it as little as possible," said practical Ottilia. "Don't seem to avoid the subject, but manage to do so in reality."

"Shall you order the tea-service?" asked Frau von Walden.

"I hardly think so. I am out of conceit of it somehow," I said. "And it might remind Nora of the blue paper parcel. I think I shall give the cup and saucer to my sister."

And on my return to England I did so.

Two years later. A very different scene from quaint old Kronberg, or still more from the dreary "Katze" at Silberbach. We are in England now, though not at our own home. We are staying, my children and I—two older girls than little Nora, and Nora herself, though hardly now to be described as "little"—with my sister. Reggie is there too, but naturally not much heard of, for it is the summer holidays, and the weather is delightful. It is August again—a typical August afternoon—though a trifle too hot perhaps for some people.

"This time two years ago, mamma," said Margaret, my eldest daughter, "you were in Germany with Nora and Reggie. What a long summer that seemed! It is so much nicer to be all together."

"I should like to go to Kronberg and all those queer places," said Lily, the second girl; "especially to the place where Nora saw the ghost."

"I am quite sure you would not wish to stay there," I replied. "It is curious that you should speak of it just now. I was thinking of it this morning. It was just two years yesterday that it happened."

We were sitting at afternoon tea on the lawn outside the drawing-room window—my sister, her husband, Margaret, Lily, and I. Nora was with the schoolroom party inside.

"How queer!" said Lily.

"You don't think Nora has thought of it?" I asked.

"Oh no, I am sure she hasn't," said Margaret. "I think it has grown vague to her now. You know she spoke about it to us when she first came home. You had prepared us, you remember, mamma, and told us not to make too much of it. The first year after, she did think of it. She told me she was dreadfully frightened all that day for fear he should appear again. But since then I think she has gradually forgotten it."

"She is a very sensible child," said my sister. "And she is especially kind and sympathising with any of the little ones who seem timid. I found her sitting beside Charlie the other night for ever so long because he heard an owl hooting outside, and was frightened."

Just then a servant came out of the house, and said something to my brother-in-law. He got up at once.

"It is Mr. Grenfell," he said to his wife, "and a friend with him. Shall I bring them out here?"

"Yes, it would really be a pity to go into the house again—it is so nice out here," she replied. And her husband went to meet his guests.

He appeared again in a minute or two, stepping out through the low window of the drawing-room, accompanied by the two gentlemen.

Mr. Grenfell was a young man living in the neighbourhood, whom we had known from his boyhood; the stranger he introduced to us as Sir Robert Masters. He was a middle-aged man, with a quiet, gentle bearing and expression.

"You will have some tea?" said my sister, after the first few words of greeting had passed. Mr. Grenfell declined. His friend accepted.

"Go into the drawing-room, Lily, please, and ring for a cup and saucer," said her aunt, noting the deficiency. "There was an extra one, but some one has poured milk into the saucer. It surely can't have been you, Mark, for Tiny?" she went on, turning to her husband. "You shouldn't let a dog drink out of anything we drink out of ourselves."

My brother-in-law looked rather comically penitent; he did not attempt to deny the charge.

"Only, my dear, you must allow," he pleaded, "that we do not drink our tea out of the saucers."

On what trifling links hang sometimes important results! Had it not been for Mark's transgressing in the matter of Tiny's milk we should never have learnt the circumstances which give to this simple relation of facts—valueless in itself—such interest, speculative and suggestive only, I am aware, as it may be found to possess.

Lily, in the meantime, had disappeared. But more quickly than it would have taken her to ring the bell, and await the servant's response to the summons, she was back again, carrying something carefully in her hand.

"Aunt," she said, "is it not a good idea? As you have a tea-spoon—I don't suppose Tiny used the spoon, did he?—I thought, instead of ringing for another, I would bring out the ghost-cup for Sir Robert. It is only fair to use it for once, poor thing, and just as we have been speaking about it. Oh, I assure you it is not dusty," as my sister regarded it dubiously. "It was inside the cabinet."

"Still, all the same, a little hot water will do it no harm," said her aunt—"provided, that is to say, that Sir Robert has no objection to drink out of a cup with such a name attached to it?"

"On the contrary," replied he, "I shall think it an honour. But you will, I trust, explain the meaning of the name to me? It puzzles me more than if it were a piece of ancient china—a great-great-grandmother's cup, for instance. For I see it is not old, though it is very pretty, and, I suppose, uncommon?"

There was a slight tone of hesitation about the last word which struck me.

"I have no doubt my sister will be ready to tell you all there is to tell. It was she who gave me the cup," replied the lady of the house.

Then Sir Robert turned to me. Looking at him full in the face I saw that there was a thoughtful, far-seeing look in his eyes, which redeemed his whole appearance from the somewhat commonplace gentlemanliness which was all I had before observed about him.

"I am greatly interested in these subjects," he said. "It would be very kind of you to tell me the whole."

I did so, more rapidly and succinctly of course than I have done here. It is not easy to play the part of narrator, with five or six pairs of eyes fixed upon you, more especially when the owners of several of them have heard the story a good many times before, and are quick to observe the slightest discrepancy, however unintentional. "There is, you see, very little to tell," I said in conclusion, "only there is always a certain amount of impressiveness about any experience of the kind when related at first hand."

"Undoubtedly so," Sir Robert replied. "Thank you very much indeed for telling it me."

He spoke with perfect courtesy, but with a slight absence of manner, his eyes fixed rather dreamily on the cup in his hand. He seemed as if trying to recall or recollect something.

"There should be a sequel to that story," said Mr. Grenfell.

"That's what I say," said Margaret eagerly. "It will be too stupid if we never hear any more. But that is always the way with modern ghost stories—there is no sense or meaning in them. The ghosts appear to people who never knew them, who take no interest in them, as it were, and then they have nothing to say—there is no dénouement, it is all purposeless."

Sir Robert looked at her thoughtfully.

"There is a good deal in what you say," he replied. "But I think there is a good deal also to be deduced from the very fact you speak of, for it is a fact. I believe what you call the meaninglessness and purposelessness—the arbitrariness, one may say, of modern experiences of the kind are the surest proofs of their authenticity. Long ago people mixed up fact and fiction, their imaginations ran riot and on some very slight foundation—often, no doubt, genuine, though slight—they built up a very complete and thrilling 'ghost story.' Nowadays we consider and philosophise, we want to get to the root and reason of things, and we are more wary of exaggeration. The result is that the only genuine ghosts are most unsatisfactory beings; they appear without purpose, and seem to be what, in fact, I believe they almost always are, irresponsible, purposeless will-o'-the-wisps. But from these I would separate the class of ghost stories the best attested and most impressive—those that have to do with the moment of death; any vision that appears just at or about that time has generally more meaning in it, I think you will find. Such ghosts appear for a reason, if no other than that of intense affection, which draws them near those from whom they are to be separated."

We listened attentively to this long explanation, though by no means fully understanding it.

"I have often heard," I said, "that the class of ghost stories you speak of are the only thoroughly authenticated ones, and I think one is naturally more inclined to believe in them than in any others. But I confess I do not in the least understand what you mean by speaking of other ghosts as 'will-o'-the-wisps.' You don't mean that though at the moment of death there is a real being—the soul, in fact, as distinct from the body, in which all but materialists believe—that this has no permanent existence, but melts away by degrees till it becomes an irresponsible, purposeless nothing—a will-o'-the-wisp in fact? I think I heard of some theory of the kind lately in a French book, but it shocked and repelled me so that I tried to forget it. Just as well, better, believe that we are nothing but our bodies, and that all is over when we die. Surely you don't mean what I say?"

"God forbid," said Sir Robert, with a fervency which startled while it reassured me. "It is my profound belief that not only we are something more than our bodies, but that our bodies are the merest outer dress of the real ourselves. It is also my profound belief that at death we—the real we—either enter at once into a state of rest temporarily, or, in some cases—for I do not believe in any cut-and-dry rule independently of individual considerations—are privileged at once to enter upon a sphere of nobler and purer labour," and here the speaker's eyes glowed with a light that was not of this world. "Is it then the least probable, is it not altogether discordant with our 'common sense'—a Divine gift which we may employ fearlessly—to suppose that these real 'selves,' freed from the weight of their discarded garments, would leave either their blissful repose, or, still less, their new activities, to come back to wander about, purposelessly and aimlessly, in this world, at best only perplexing and alarming such as may perceive them? Is it not contrary to all we find of the wisdom and reasonableness of such laws as we do know something about?"

"I have often thought so," I said, "and hitherto this has led me to be very sceptical about all ghost stories."

"But they are often true—so far as they go," he replied. "Our natures are much more complex than we ourselves understand or realise. I cannot now go at all thoroughly into the subject, but to give you a rough idea of my will-o'-the-wisp theory—can you not imagine a sort of shadow, or echo of ourselves, lingering about the scenes we have frequented on this earth, which under certain very rare conditions—the state of the atmosphere among others—may be perceptible to those still 'clothed upon' with this present body? To attempt a simile, I might suggest the perfume that lingers when the flowers are thrown away, the smoke that gradually dissolves after the lamp is extinguished! This is very, very loosely and roughly the sort of thing I mean by my 'will-o'-the-wisps.'"

"I don't like it at all," said Margaret, though she smiled a little. "I think I should be more frightened if I saw that kind of ghost—I mean if I thought it that kind—than by a good, honest, old-fashioned one, who knew what it was about and meant to come."

"But you have just said," he objected, "that they never do seem to know what they are about. Besides, why should you be frightened?—our fears, ourselves in fact—are the only thing we really need be frightened of—our weaknesses and ignorances and folly. There was great truth in that rather ghastly story of Calderra's, allegory though it is, about the man whose evil genius was himself; have you read it?"

We all shook our heads.

"It is ignorance that frightens us," he went on. "In this instance think of the appearances we are speaking of as almost of the nature of a photograph, or the reflection in a looking-glass. I daresay we should have been terrified by these, had we not grown used to them, did we not know what they are.

Somebody said lately what appalling things we should think our own shadows, if we had suddenly for the first time become aware of them."

"I don't mind so much," said Margaret, "when you speak of ghosts as a sort of photograph. But—" she hesitated.

"Pray say what you are thinking."

"Just now when you said how incredible it was that real souls should return to this earth, you only spoke of good people, did you not?"

In his turn Sir Robert hesitated.

"It is difficult to draw a line even in thought between good and bad people," he said, "and, thank God, it is not for us to do so. 'To my Maker alone I stand or I fall.' There is evil in the best; there is, I would fain hope," but here his face grew grave and sad, "good in the worst. But even allowing that we could draw the line, is it likely that the bad, even those who have all but lost the last spark, who don't want to be good, is it likely that they, if, as we must believe, under Divine control, would be allowed to leave their new life of punishment—punishment in the sense of correction, mind you—to come back here, wasting their time, one may say, to frighten perfectly innocent people for no purpose? No, I think I am quite consistent. Only try to get rid of all fears—that is what we can all do. But really I should apologise for all this lecture;" and he was turning to me with a smile, when his eyes fell on the cup which he had replaced on the table.

"I cannot get over the impression that I have seen that cup—no, not that cup, but one just like it, before. Not long ago, I fancy," he said.

"Oh, you must let us know if you find out anything," we all exclaimed.

"I certainly shall do so," he said, and a few minutes afterwards he and Mr. Grenfell took their leave.

But I had time for a word or two with the latter out of hearing of the others.

"Who is Sir Robert Masters?" I asked. "Have you known him long? He is a very uncommon and impressive sort of man."

"Yes, I thought you would like him. I have not personally known him long, but he is an old friend of friends of ours. He is of good family, an old baronetcy, but he is not much known in fashionable society. He travels a great deal, or has done so rather, and people say he has 'peculiar ideas,' though that would not go against him in the world. Peculiar ideas, or the cant of them, are rather the fashion it seems to me! But there is no cant about him. And whatever his ideas are," went on young Grenfell warmly, "he is one of the best men I ever knew. He has settled down for some years, and devotes his whole life to doing good, but so quietly and unostentatiously that no one knows how much he does, and others get the credit of it very often."

That was all I heard.

I have never seen Sir Robert again. Still I have by no means arrived yet at the end of my so-called ghost story.

The cup and saucer were carefully washed and replaced in the glass-doored cabinet. The summer gradually waned, and we all returned to our own home. It was at a considerable distance from my sister's, and we met each other principally in the summer time. So, though I did not forget Sir Robert Masters, or his somewhat strange conversation, amid the crowd of daily interests and pleasures, duties and cares, none of the incidents I have here recorded were much in my mind, and but that I had while still in Germany carefully noted the details of all bearing directly or indirectly on "Nora's ghost," as we had come to call it—though it was but rarely alluded to before the child herself—I should not now have been able to give them with circumstantiality.

Fully fifteen months after the visit to my sister, during which we had met Sir Robert, the whole was suddenly and unexpectedly recalled to my memory. Mark and Nora the elder—my sister, that is,—were in their turn staying with us, when one morning at breakfast the post brought for the latter an unusually bulky and important-looking letter. She opened it, glanced at an outer sheet enclosing several pages in a different handwriting, and passed it on to me.

"We must read the rest together," she said in a low voice, glancing at the children, who were at the table. "How interesting it will be!"

The sheet she had handed to me was a short note from Mr. Grenfell. It was dated from some place in Norway where he was fishing, and from whence he had addressed the whole packet to my sister's own home, not knowing of her absence.

"My dear Mrs. Daventry"—it began—"The enclosed will have been a long time of reaching its real destination, for it is, as you will see, really intended for your sister. No doubt it will interest you too, as it has done me, though I am too matter-of-fact and prosaic to enter into such things much. Still it is curious. Please keep the letter; I am sure my friend intends you to do so.

"Yours very truly,

"Ralph Grenfell."

The manuscript enclosed was, of course, from Sir Robert himself. It was in the form of a letter to young Grenfell; and after explaining that he thought it better to write to him, not having my address, he plunged into the real object of his communication.

"You will not," he said, "have forgotten the incident of the 'ghost-cup,' in the summer of last year, and the curious story your friend was so good as to tell us about it. You may remember—Mrs. — will, I am sure, do so—my strong impression that I had recently seen one like it. After I left you I could not get this feeling out of my head. It is always irritating not to be able, figuratively speaking, 'to lay your hand' on a recollection, and in this instance I really wanted to get the clue, as it might lead to some sort of 'explanation' of the little girl's strange experience. I cudgelled my brains, but all to no purpose; I went over in memory all the houses at which I had visited within a certain space of time; I made lists of all the people I knew interested in 'china,' ancient or modern, and likely to possess specimens of it. But all in vain. All I got for my pains was that people began to think I was developing a new crotchet, or, as I heard one lady say to another, not knowing I was within earshot, 'the poor man must be a little off his head, though till now I have always denied it. But the revulsion from benevolent schemes to china-collecting shows it only too plainly.' So I thought I had better leave off cross-questioning my 'collecting' friends about porcelain and faïence, German ware in particular. And after a while I thought no more about it. Two months ago I had occasion to make a journey to the north—the same journey and to stay at the same house where I have been four or five times since I saw the 'ghost-cup.' But this was what happened this time. There is a junction by which one must pass on this journey. I generally manage to suit my trains so as to avoid waiting there, but this is not always feasible. This time I found that an hour at the junction was inevitable. There is a very good refreshment room there, kept by very civil, decent people. They knew me by sight, and after I had had a cup of tea they proposed to me, as they have done before, to wait in their little parlour just off the public room. 'It would be quieter and more comfortable,' said either the mother or the daughter who manage the concern. I thanked them, and settled myself in an arm-chair with my book, when, looking up—there on the mantelpiece stood the fellow cup—the identical shape, pattern, and colour! It all flashed into my mind then. I had made this journey just before going into your neighbourhood last year, and had waited in this little parlour just as this time.

"'Where did you get that cup, Mrs. Smith?' I asked.

"There were two or three rather pretty bits of china about. The good woman was pleased at my noticing it.

"'Yes, sir. Isn't it pretty? I've rather a fancy for china. That cup was sent me by my niece. She said she'd picked it up somewhere—at a sale, I think. It's foreign, sir; isn't it?'

"'Yes, German. But can't you find out where your niece got it?' for at the word 'sale' my hopes fell.

"'I can ask her. I shall be writing to her this week,' she replied; and she promised to get any information she could for me within a fortnight, by which time I expected to pass that way again. I did so, and Mrs. Smith proved as good as her word. The niece had got the cup from a friend of hers, an auctioneer, and he, not she, had got it at a sale. But he was away from home—she could hear nothing more at present. She gave his address, however, and assurances that he was very good-natured and would gladly put the gentleman in the way of getting china like it, if it was to be got. He would be home by the middle of the month. It was now the middle of the month. The auctioneer's town was not above a couple of hours off my line. Perhaps you will all laugh at me when I tell you that I went those two hours out of my way, arriving at the town late that night and putting up at a queer old inn—worth going to see for itself—on purpose to find the man of the hammer. I found him. He was very civil, though rather mystified. He remembered the cup perfectly, but there was no chance of getting any like it where it came from!

"'And where was that?' I asked eagerly.

"'At a sale some miles from here, about four years ago,' he replied. 'It was the sale of the furniture and plate, and everything, in fact, of a widow lady. She had some pretty china, for she had a fancy for it. That cup was not of much value; it was quite modern. I bought it in for a trifle. I gave it to Miss Cross, and she sent it to her aunt, as you know. As for getting any like it—'

"But I interrupted him by assuring him I did not wish that, but that I had reasons for wanting some information about the person who, I believed, had bought the cup. 'Nothing to do any harm to any one,'

I said; 'a matter of feeling. A similar cup had been bought by a person I was interested in, and I feared that person was dead.'

"The auctioneer's face cleared. He fancied he began to understand me.

"'I am afraid you are right, sir, if the person you mean was young Mr. Paulet, the lady's son. You may have met him on his travels? His death was very sad, I believe. It killed his mother, they say—she never looked up after; and as she had no near relative to follow her, everything was sold. I remember I was told all that, at the sale, and it seemed to me particularly sad, even though one comes across many sad things in our line of business.'

"'Do you remember the particulars of Mr. Paulet's death?' I asked.

"'Only that it happened suddenly—somewhere in foreign parts. I did not know the family till I was asked to take charge of the sale,' he replied.

"'Could you possibly get any details for me? I feel sure it is the same Mr. Paulet,' I said boldly.

"The auctioneer considered.

"'Perhaps I can. I rather think a former servant of theirs is still in the neighbourhood,' he replied.

"I thanked him and left him my address, to which he promised to write. I felt it was perhaps better not to pursue my inquiries further in person; it might lead to annoyance, or possibly to gossip about the dead, which I detest. I jotted down some particulars for the auctioneer's guidance, and went on my way. That was a fortnight ago. To-day I have his answer, which I transcribe:—

"'Sir—The servant I spoke of could not tell me very much, as she was not long in the late Mrs. Paulet's service. To hear more, she says, you must apply to the relations of the family. Young Mr. Paulet was tall and fair and very nice-looking. His mother and he were deeply attached to each other. He travelled a good deal and used to bring her home lots of pretty things. He met his death in some part of Germany where there are forests, for though it was thought at first he had died of heart disease, the doctors proved he had been struck by lightning, and his body was found in the forest, and the papers on him showed who he was. The body was sent home to be buried, and all that was found with it; a knapsack and its contents, among which was the cup I bought at the sale. His death was about the middle of August 18—. I shall be glad if this information is of any service.'

"This," continued Sir Robert's own letter, "is all I have been able to learn. There does not seem to have been the very slightest suspicion of foul play, nor do I think it the least likely there was any ground for such. Young Paulet probably died some way farther in the forest than Silberbach, and it is even possible the surly landlord never heard of it. It might be worth while to inquire about it should your friends ever be there again. If I should be in the neighbourhood I certainly should do so; the whole coincidences are very striking."

Then followed apologies for the length of his letter which he had been betrayed into by his anxiety to tell all there was to tell. In return he asked Mr. Grenfell to obtain from me certain dates and particulars as he wished to note them down. It was the 18th of August on which "Nora's ghost" had appeared—just two years after the August of the poor young man's death!

There was also a postscript to Sir Robert's letter, in which he said, "I think, in Mrs. —'s place, I would say nothing to the little girl of what we have discovered."

And I have never done so.

This is all I have to tell. I offer no suggestions, no theories in explanation of the facts. Those who, like Sir Robert Masters, are able and desirous to treat such subjects scientifically or philosophically will doubtless form their own. I cannot say that I find his theory a perfectly satisfactory one, perhaps I do not sufficiently understand it, but I have tried to give it in his own words. Should this matter-of-fact relation of a curious experience meet his eyes, I am sure he will forgive my having brought him into it. Besides, it is not likely that he would be recognised; men, and women too, of "peculiar ideas," sincere investigators and honest searchers after truth, as well as their superficial plagiarists, being by no means rare in these days.

IV

THE STORY OF THE RIPPLING TRAIN

A TRUE GHOST STORY

"Let's tell ghost stories, then," said Gladys.

"Aren't you tired of them? One hears nothing else nowadays. And they're all 'authentic,' really vouched for, only you never see the person who saw or heard or felt the ghost. It is always somebody's sister or cousin, or friend's friend," objected young Mrs. Snowdon, another of the guests at the Quarries.

"I don't know that that is quite a reasonable ground for discrediting them en masse," said her husband. "It is natural enough, indeed inevitable, that the principal or principals in such cases should be much more rarely come across than the stories themselves. A hundred people can repeat the story, but the author, or rather hero, of it, can't be in a hundred places at once. You don't disbelieve in any other statement or narrative merely because you have never seen the prime mover in it?"

"But I didn't say I discredited them on that account," said Mrs. Snowdon. "You take one up so, Archie. I'm not logical and reasonable; I don't pretend to be. If I meant anything, it was that a ghost story would have a great pull over other ghost stories if one could see the person it happened to. One does get rather provoked at never coming across him or her," she added a little petulantly.

She was tired; they were all rather tired, for it was the first evening since the party had assembled at the large country house known as "the Quarries" on which there was not to be dancing, with the additional fatigue of "ten miles there and ten back again"; and three or four evenings of such doings without intermission tell even on the young and vigorous.

To-night various less energetic ways of passing the evening had been proposed,—music, games, reading aloud, recitation,—none had found favour in everybody's sight, and now Gladys Lloyd's proposal that they should "tell ghost stories" seemed likely to fall flat also.

For a moment or two no one answered Mrs. Snowdon's last remarks. Then, somewhat to everybody's surprise, the young daughter of the house turned to her mother.

"Mamma," she said, "don't be vexed with me—I know you warned me once to be careful how I spoke of it; but wouldn't it be nice if Uncle Paul would tell us his ghost story? And then, Mrs. Snowdon," she went on, "you could always say you had heard one ghost story at or from—which should I say?—headquarters."

Lady Denholme glanced round half nervously before she replied.

"Locally speaking, it would not be at headquarters, Nina," she said. "The Quarries was not the scene of your uncle's ghost story. But I almost think it is better not to speak about it—I am not sure that he would like it mentioned, and he will be coming in a moment. He had only a note to write."

"I do wish he would tell it to us," said Nina regretfully. "Don't you think, mamma, I might just run to the study and ask him, and if he did not like the idea he might say so to me, and no one would seem to know anything about it? Uncle Paul is so kind—I'm never afraid of asking him any favour."

"Thank you, Nina, for your good opinion of me; you see there is no rule without exceptions; listeners do sometimes hear pleasant things of themselves," said Mr. Marischal, as he at that moment came round the screen which half concealed the doorway. "What is the special favour you were thinking of asking me?"

Nina looked rather taken aback.

"How softly you opened the door, Uncle Paul," she said. "I would not have spoken of you if I had known you were there."

"But after all you were saying no harm," observed her brother Michael. "And for my part I don't believe Uncle Paul would mind our asking him what we were speaking of."

"What was it?" asked Mr. Marischal. "I think, as I have heard so much, you may as well tell me the whole."

"It was only—" began Nina, but her mother interrupted her.

"I have told Nina not to speak of it, Paul," she said anxiously; "but—it was only that all these young people are talking about ghost stories, and they want you to tell them your own strange experience. You must not be vexed with them."

"Vexed!" said Mr. Marischal, "not in the least." But for a moment or two he said no more, and even pretty, spoilt Mrs. Snowdon looked a little uneasy.

"You shouldn't have persisted, Nina," she whispered.

Mr. Marischal must have had unusually quick ears. He looked up and smiled.

"I really don't mind telling you all there is to hear," he said. "At one time I had a sort of dislike to mentioning the story, for the sake of others. The details would have led to its being recognised—and it might have been painful. But there is no one now living to whom it would matter—you know," he added, turning to his sister; "her husband is dead too."

Lady Denholme shook her head.

"No," she said, "I did not hear."

"Yes," said her brother, "I saw his death in the papers last year. He had married again, I believe. There is not now, therefore, any reason why I should not tell the story, if it will interest you," he went on, turning to the others. "And there is not very much to tell. Not worth making such a preamble about. It was—let me see—yes, it must be nearly fifteen years ago."

"Wait a moment, Uncle Paul," said Nina. "Yes, that's all right, Gladys. You and I will hold each other's hands, and pinch hard if we get very frightened."

"Thank you," Miss Lloyd replied. "On the whole I should prefer for you not to hold my hand."

"But I won't pinch you so as to hurt," said Nina reassuringly; "and it isn't as if we were in the dark."

"Shall I turn down the lamps?" asked Mr. Snowdon.

"No, no," exclaimed his wife.

"There really is nothing frightening—scarcely even 'creepy,' in my story at all," said Mr. Marischal, half apologetically. "You make me feel like an impostor."

"Oh no, Uncle Paul, don't say that. It is all my fault for interrupting," said Nina. "Now go on, please. I have Gladys's hand all the same," she added sotto voce, "it's just as well to be prepared."

"Well, then," began Mr. Marischal once more, "it must be nearly fifteen years ago; and I had not seen her for fully ten years before that again! I was not thinking of her in the least; in a sense I had really forgotten her: she had quite gone out of my life; that always struck me as a very curious point in the story," he added parenthetically.

"Won't you tell us who 'she' was, Uncle Paul?" asked Nina half shyly.

"Oh yes, I was going to do so. I am not skilled in story-telling, you see. She was, at the time I first knew her—at the only time, indeed, that I knew her—a very sweet and attractive girl, named Maud Bertram. She was very pretty—more than pretty, for she had remarkably regular features—her profile was always admired, and a tall and graceful figure. And she was a bright and happy creature too; that, perhaps, was almost her greatest charm. You will wonder—I see the question hovering on your lips, Miss Lloyd, and on yours too, Mrs. Snowdon—why, if I admired her and liked her so much, I did not go further. And I will tell you frankly that I did not because I dared not. I had then no prospect of being able to marry for years to come, and I was not very young. I was already nearly thirty, and Maud was quite ten years younger. I was wise enough and old enough to realise the situation thoroughly, and to be on my guard."

"And Maud?" asked Mrs. Snowdon.

"She was surrounded by admirers; it seemed to me then that it would have been insufferable conceit to have even asked myself if it could matter to her. It was only in the light of after events that the possibility of my having been mistaken occurred to me. And I don't even now see that I could have acted otherwise—" Here Uncle Paul sighed a little. "We were the best of friends. She knew that I admired her, and she seemed to take a frank pleasure in its being so. I had always hoped that she really liked and trusted me as a friend, but no more. The last time I saw her was just before I started for Portugal, where I remained three years. When I returned to London Maud had been married for two years, and had gone straight out to India on her marriage, and except by some few friends who had known us both intimately, I seldom heard her mentioned. And time passed. I cannot say I had exactly forgotten her, but she was not much or often in my thoughts. I was a busy and much-absorbed man, and life had proved a serious matter to me. Now and then some passing resemblance would recall her to my mind—once especially when I had been asked to look in to see the young wife of one of my cousins in her court-dress; something in her figure and bearing brought back Maud to my memory, for it was thus, in full dress, that I had last seen her, and thus perhaps, unconsciously, her image had remained photographed on my brain. But as far as I can recollect at the time when the occurrence I am going to relate to you happened, I had not been thinking of Maud Bertram for months. I was in London just then, staying with my brother, my eldest brother, who had been married for several years, and lived in our own old town-house in — Square. It was in April, a clear spring day, with no fog or half-lights about, and it was not yet four o'clock in the afternoon—not very ghost-like circumstances, you will admit. I had come home early from my club—it was a sort of holiday-time with me just then for a few weeks—intending to get some letters written which had been on my mind for some days, and I had sauntered into the library, a pleasant, fair-sized room lined with books, on the first-floor. Before setting to work I sat down for a moment or two in an easy-chair by the fire, for it was still cool enough weather to make a fire desirable, and began thinking over my letters. No thought, no shadow of a thought of my old friend Miss Bertram was present with me; of that I am perfectly certain. The door was on the same side of the room as the fireplace; as I sat there, half facing the fire, I also half faced the door. I had not shut it properly on coming in—I had only closed it without turning the handle—and I did not feel surprised when it slowly and noiselessly swung open, till it stood right out into the room, concealing the actual doorway from my view. You will perhaps understand the position better if you think of the door as just then acting like a screen to the doorway. From where I sat I could not have seen any one entering the room till he or she had got beyond the door itself. I glanced up, half expecting to see some one come in, but there was no one; the door had swung open of itself. For the moment I sat on, with only the vague thought passing through my mind, 'I must shut it before I begin to write.'

"But suddenly I found my eyes fixing themselves on the carpet; something had come within their range of vision, compelling their attention in a mechanical sort of way. What was it?

"'Smoke,' was my first idea. 'Can there be anything on fire?' But I dismissed the notion almost as soon as it suggested itself. The something, faint and shadowy, that came slowly rippling itself in as it were beyond the dark wood of the open door, was yet too material for 'smoke.' My next idea was a curious one. 'It looks like soapy water,' I said to myself; 'can one of the housemaids have been scrubbing, and upset a pail on the stairs?' For the stair to the next floor almost faced the library door. But—no; I rubbed my eyes and looked again; the soapy water theory gave way. The wavy something that kept gliding, rippling in, gradually assumed a more substantial appearance. It was—yes, I suddenly became convinced of it—it was ripples of soft silken stuff, creeping in as if in some mysterious way unfolded or unrolled, not jerkily or irregularly, but glidingly and smoothly, like little wavelets on the sea-shore.

"And I sat there and gazed. 'Why did you not jump up and look behind the door to see what it was?' you may reasonably ask. That question I cannot answer. Why I sat still, as if bewitched, or under some irresistible influence, I cannot tell, but so it was.

"And it—came always rippling in, till at last it began to rise as it still came on, and I saw that a figure—a tall, graceful woman's figure—was slowly advancing, backwards of course, into the room, and that the waves of pale silk—a very delicate shade of pearly gray I think it must have been—were in fact the lower portion of a long court-train, the upper part of which hung in deep folds from the lady's waist. She moved in—I cannot describe the motion, it was not like ordinary walking or stepping backwards—till the whole of her figure and the clear profile of her face and head were distinctly visible, and when at last she stopped and stood there full in my view just, but only just beyond the door, I saw—it came upon me like a flash—that she was no stranger to me, this mysterious visitant! I recognised, unchanged it seemed to me since the day, ten years ago, when I had last seen her, the beautiful features of Maud Bertram."

Mr. Marischal stopped a moment. Nobody spoke. Then he went on again.

"I should not have said 'unchanged.' There was one great change in the sweet face. You remember my telling you that one of my girl-friend's greatest charms was her bright sunny happiness—she never seemed gloomy or depressed or dissatisfied, seldom even pensive. But in this respect the face I sat there gazing at was utterly unlike Maud Bertram's. Its expression, as she—or 'it'—stood there looking, not towards me, but out beyond, as if at some one or something outside the doorway, was of the profoundest sadness. Anything so sad I had never seen in a human face, and I trust I never may. But I sat on, as motionless almost as she, gazing at her fixedly, with no desire, no power perhaps, to move or approach more nearly to the phantom. I was not in the least frightened. I knew it was a phantom, but I felt paralysed, and as if I myself had somehow got outside of ordinary conditions. And there I sat—staring at Maud, and there she stood, gazing before her with that terrible, unspeakable sadness in her face, which, even though I felt no fear, seemed to freeze me with a kind of unutterable pity.

"I don't know how long I had sat thus, or how long I might have continued to sit there, almost as if in a trance, when suddenly I heard the front-door bell ring. It seemed to awaken me. I started up and glanced round, half-expecting that I should find the vision dispelled. But no; she was still there, and I sank back into my seat just as I heard my brother coming quickly upstairs. He came towards the library, and seeing the door wide open walked in, and I, still gazing, saw his figure pass through that of the woman in the doorway as you may walk through a wreath of mist or smoke—only, don't misunderstand me, the figure of Maud till that moment had had nothing unsubstantial about it. She had looked to me, as she stood there, literally and exactly like a living woman—the shade of her dress, the colour of her hair, the few ornaments she wore, all were as defined and clear as yours, Nina, at the present moment, and remained so, or perhaps became so again as soon as my brother was well within the room. He came forward addressing me by name, but I answered him in a whisper, begging him to be silent and to sit down on the seat opposite me for a moment or two. He did so, though he was taken aback by my strange manner, for I still kept my eyes fixed on the door. I had a queer consciousness that if I looked away it would fade, and I wanted to keep cool and see what would happen. I asked Herbert in a low voice if he saw nothing, but though he mechanically followed the direction of my eyes, he shook his head in bewilderment. And for a moment or two he remained thus. Then I began to notice that the figure was growing less clear, as if it were receding, yet without growing smaller to the sight; it grew fainter and vaguer, the colours grew hazy. I rubbed my eyes once or twice with a half idea that my long watching was making them misty, but it was not so. My eyes were not at fault—slowly but surely Maud Bertram, or her ghost, melted away, till all trace of her had gone. I saw again the familiar pattern of the carpet where she had stood and the objects of the room that had been hidden by her draperies—all again in the most commonplace way, but she was gone, quite gone.

"Then Herbert, seeing me relax my intense gaze, began to question me. I told him exactly what I have told you. He answered, as every "common-sensible" person of course would, that it was strange, but that such things did happen sometimes and were classed by the wise under the head of 'optical delusions.' I was not well, perhaps, he suggested. Been over-working? Had I not better see a doctor? But I shook my head. I was quite well, and I said so. And perhaps he was right, it might be an optical delusion only. I had never had any experience of such things.

"'All the same,' I said, 'I shall mark down the date.'

"Herbert laughed and said that was what people always did in such cases. If he knew where Mrs. — then was he would write to her, just for the fun of the thing, and ask her to be so good as to look up her diary, if she kept one, and let us know what she had been doing on that particular day—'the 6th of April, isn't it?' he said—when I would have it her wraith had paid me a visit. I let him talk. It seemed to remove the strange painful impression—painful because of that terrible sadness in the sweet face. But we neither of us knew where she was, we scarcely remembered her married name! And so there was nothing to be done—except what I did at once in spite of Herbert's rallying, to mark down the day and hour with scrupulous exactness in my diary.

"Time passed. I had not forgotten my strange experience, but of course the impression of it lessened by degrees till it seemed more like a curious dream than anything more real, when one day I did hear of poor Maud again. 'Poor' Maud I cannot help calling her. I heard of her indirectly, and probably, but for the sadness of her story, I should never have heard it at all. It was a friend of her husband's family who had mentioned the circumstances in the hearing of a friend of mine, and one day something brought round the conversation to old times, and he startled me by suddenly inquiring if I remembered Maud Bertram. I said, of course I did. Did he know anything of her? And then he told me.

"She was dead—she had died some months ago after a long and trying illness, the result of a terrible accident. She had caught fire one evening when dressed for some grand entertainment or other, and though her injuries did not seem likely to be fatal at the time, she had never recovered the shock.

"'She was so pretty,' my friend said, 'and one of the saddest parts of it was that I hear she was terrifically disfigured, and she took this most sadly to heart. The right side of her face was utterly ruined, and the sight of the right eye lost, though, strange to say, the left side entirely escaped, and seeing her in profile one would have had no notion of what had happened. Was it not sad? She was such a sweet, bright creature.'

"I did not tell him my story, for I did not want it chattered about, but a strange sort of shiver ran through me at his words. It was the left side of her face only that the wraith of my poor friend had allowed me to see."

"Oh, Uncle Paul!" exclaimed Nina.

"And—as to the dates?" inquired Mr. Snowdon.

"I never knew the exact date of the accident," said Mr. Marischal, "but that of her death was fully six months after I had seen her. And in my own mind, I have never made any doubt that it was at or about, probably a short time after, the accident, that she came to me. It seemed a kind of appeal for sympathy—and—a farewell also, poor child."

They all sat silent for some little time, and then Mr. Marischal got up and went off to his own quarters, saying something vaguely about seeing if his letters had gone.

"What a touching story!" said Gladys Lloyd. "I am afraid, after all, it has been more painful than he realised for Mr. Marischal to tell it. Did you know anything of Maud's husband, dear Lady Denholme? Was he kind to her? Was she happy?"

"We never heard much about her married life," her hostess replied. "But I have no reason to think she was unhappy. Her husband married again two or three years after her death, but that says nothing."

"N—no," said Nina. "All the same, mamma, I am sure she really did love Uncle Paul very much,—much more than he had any idea of. Poor Maud!"

"And he has never married," added Gladys.

"No," said Lady Denholme, "but there have been many practical difficulties in the way of his doing so. He has had a most absorbingly busy life, and now that he is more at leisure he feels himself too old to form new ties."

"But," persisted Nina, "if he had had any idea at the time that Maud cared for him so?"

"Ah well," Lady Denholme allowed, "in that case, in spite of the practical difficulties, things would probably have been different."

And again Nina repeated softly, "Poor Maud!"

Mary Louisa Molesworth - A Concise Bibliography
Lover And Husband (1869)
Cicely (1874)
Tell Me A Story (1875),
Carrots: Just A Little Boy (1876)
The Cuckoo Clock (1877)
A Christmas Fairy & Other Stories (1878)
Hathercourt Rectory (3 volumes; 1878)
The Tapestry Room; A Child's Romance (1879)
A Christmas Child: A Sketch Of A Boy-Life (1880)
Miss Bouverie: A Novel (1880)
The Adventures of Herr Baby (1881)

Grandmother Dear; A Book For Boys And Girls (1882)
Rosy (1882)
The Boys & I; A Child's Story For Children (1883)
Two Little Waifs (1883)
Christmas Tree Land (1886)
Us: An Old-Fashioned Story (1886)
Jack Frost's Little Prisoners: A Collection of Stories (1887), one of several contributors.
Little Miss Peggy: Only A Nursery Story (1887)
The Palace In The Garden (1887)
A Christmas Posy (1888)
Four Ghost Stories (1888)
French Life In Letters (1889)
The Rectory Children (1889)
Neighbours (1889) with Mary Ellen Edwards
The Green Casket & Other Stories (1890)
Family Troubles (1890)
Imogen: or, Only Eighteen (1890s)
Robin Redbreast: A Story For Girls (1890s)
The Girls and I: A Veracious History (1892)
The Man With The Pan-Pipes & Other Stories (circa 1892)
Leona (circa 1892)
The Next Door House. (1892)
The Cuckoo Clock (1893)
Four Winds Farm; and, The Children Of The Castle (2 books in 1 volume, 1893)
Mary (1893)
Nurse Heatherdale's Story; And Little Miss Peggy (1893)
Studies & Stories (1893)
My New Home (1894)
A Budget Of Christmas Tales (1895) with works by Charles Dickens and Others
The Carved Lions (1895)
Olivia, A Story For Girls (1895)
Uncanny Tales (circa 1896)
Philippa (1896)
Sheila's Mystery (1896)
The Oriel Window (1896)
Hoodie (1897)
Meg Langholme; or, The Day After Tomorrow (1897)
The Magic Nuts (1898)
The Laurel Walk (1899)
This And That: A Tale Of Two Tinies (1899)
Miss Mouse And Her Boys (1897)
The Wood Pigeons And Mary (1901) with H. R. Millar
Peterkin (1902)
Fairies - Of Sorts, (1908)
Edmeé: A Tale Of The French Revolution (1916)
Stories by Mrs. Molesworth (1922)

www.ingramcontent.com/pod-product-compliance
Lightning Source LLC
Chambersburg PA
CBHW061457170626
46811CB00004B/1551